D1146385

YESTERDAY'S ENEMY

YESTERDAY'S ENEMY

ENEMY

William Haggard

CASSELL
LONDON

CASSELL & COMPANY LIMITED
35 Red Lion Square, London WC1R 4SG
and at Sydney, Auckland, Toronto, Johannesburg,
an affiliate of
Macmillan Publishing Co, Inc,
New York

First published 1976

ISBN 0 304 29727 5

Typeset by Malvern Typesetting Services Limited
Printed in Great Britain by
Richard Clay (The Chaucer Press) Ltd
Bungay, Suffolk

F.576

1

The visitor drank some claret thoughtfully, and Colonel Charles Russell, lately Head of the Security Executive, sat and watched him do it patiently. This satrap of an alien system wasn't a man to be hurried or pestered and very few men ever dared to do so. He would come to his point in time. And a shrewd one. It could even in the end spell peace or war.

Charles Russell, in his working days, had been paid to confound this man's least project and he had something more than earned his salary. There had been rubbers which he had handsomely lost, others which he had won as handsomely. But he had never regarded the Colonel-General as in any sense a personal enemy. They had too much in common for private malice, in particular a respect for reality. Power would survive the humanist fallacy, the pipedreams of the new reformers with their comfortable private incomes behind them. It wasn't love which made the world go round and it wasn't, for that matter, naked hate. It was the ability to think politically and to see that one's orders were carried out. The General possessed these and Russell the first of them. It was the basis of their mutual respect and sometimes for something quite close to affection.

Russell sat quietly and waited in silence, reflecting that there was nothing strange in the fact that the two of them sat together. They had consulted many times before but they had done so covertly, hiding their movements in neutral countries, in steamers up and down great rivers, and twice in the Colonel-General's own capital. Once, to Russell's shame and horror, he'd been required to wear a false beard and dark glasses. But only once—he had put his foot down. There were limits to even the closest friendships.

So it wasn't strange that they sat together, only strange that they did so quite openly. There was a still efficient organization which must know of the Colonel-General's presence but it wouldn't rush to inform its masters since its masters wouldn't wish to know. The Colonel-General was far too wise to take any hand in local mischief, though God knew there was enough of that brewing, so provided he simply came and went no protest would be even considered. Some years ago most surely it would have been. But the name of today's golden calf was *détente*: nothing must be done to offend it. Charles Russell was certain the idol was hollow. It was a real measure of declining power and though it saddened him he had learnt to accept it.

They were dining in a private room of the Colonel-General's London embassy. The food was good and the wine even better. Charles Russell in turn drank some claret appreciatively. It had been carefully decanted, no bottle was visible, and Russell, though an ardent wine-lover, would have denied much expert knowledge of vintages. Just the same he would have betted a pony that this had been bottled in '62. They were really doing him very proud, but then they had the money to do so. The general standard of living was low—an enormous army saw to that, the fear of war on two fronts and adventures in space. But for the privileged there was money at all times.

. . . Perhaps there was a case, perhaps there wasn't.

Russell's host broke the silence at last and deliberately. 'West Germany,' he said, with the quiet satisfaction of a Russian whose land had been ravaged by Germans, 'is not a Sovereign State, or not yet.' His manner was solemn; it wasn't pompous.

'I'm not sure I follow.'

'You do not surprise me. I was speaking as a lawyer would and lawyers are traditionally obscure. But nevertheless the point is valid.'

'Expound,' Russell said.

'With your permission I'll do so.' The Colonel-General finished his wine; he clapped his hands for another decanter. 'A Sovereign State cannot be coerced, or rather if it is that means war. But four Powers of which your own is still one could legally act in Western Germany if the Western Germans did certain things. And I've superiors who believe that they might.'

'I'm deeper in the fog than ever.'

'Which a German nuclear bang would blow away.'

Charles Russell shook his head with decision. 'I simply don't believe it's on, the West Germans have far too much to lose. Consider.' Russell ticked it off on still muscular fingers. 'They have prosperity and a low rate of inflation. Their currency is admirably managed. They have a working class prepared to work for the extras which steady working will earn them. I don't say they've changed their basic nature—to a Russian I wouldn't propose such a heresy—but they're a very easy people to discipline and for the moment at least they've turned to wealth. It's butter before guns with a vengeance. As for their future that's in your hands in practice. Personally I'm perfectly happy to see their country divided indefinitely, and even if they went communist I doubt if you'd allow reunion.' Charles Russell shook his head again. 'They know all this and are far from stupid. They won't play silly games with forbidden arms.'

'In fact I'm not suggesting they would. . . . Some neo-Nazi sect with a grievance. . . . They steal something from the Americans or perhaps they try to make it in secret. . . . It's the plot of a dozen indifferent thrillers. I've read some of them and they make me laugh. They're not supposed to do that, you know.'

'I know they're not. They make me weep.' Charles Russell accepted a slice of Brie. 'But if you don't think that sort of nonsense is possible why are you worried ? I see you are.'

The General appeared to change the subject. 'I'm sometimes thought a sort of dictator, at least in my own small specialist field, but in practice I am no such thing. I report to my colleagues just as you did, and my colleagues consist of both hawks and doves. I apologize for the shocking cliché but for the moment it serves as well as another. And the hawks are very much present still.'

'Yes?'

'I told you I agreed with you that the West Germans will do nothing foolish.' The Colonel-General put powerful hands on the table, speaking with uncharacteristic emphasis. *'What I fear is that somebody else, not German, will frame the appearance they're doing just that.* In that case our hawks would be off the glove. They'd move in at once and unilaterally——'

'I can't pretend I'd blame them.'

'Not you. But it could very well lead to the final war and the western world cannot afford it.'

'Nor can you.'

'Just so. But you misunderstand me. In the present context we're western world too. We may have a very different system, we may think your economics childish, but putting it coarsely we've white skins too. If we make the industrialized world uninhabitable, which could happen if our hawks break their leashes and if America stands by her obligations—if that came to pass you will know who would benefit. The Chinese——'

'I admire them.'

'The Indians.'

'No.'

'Tinpot dictators in African states.'

'Anything but them,' Russell said.

'I see I am making my point. Let us move to another room for coffee.'

They settled to coffee and Caucasian brandy, and when he had taken his ration of both Charles Russell began to sum up judicially. 'All this is a matter of theory, but fascinating. Someone is going to frame the West Germans, but with what exactly I do not follow. You've said two things yourself so I'm going to repeat them. Stealing an American warhead is something out of a second-rate thriller, and making a nuclear bomb in secret is something I do not believe is possible.'

'*But if somebody rigged the appearance they were?*'

'Would anybody believe it?'

'I fear so. I wouldn't myself, or not until recently.' The General produced a newspaper cutting. 'From the only British paper I read since it's the only one left with some sense of reality.' He passed the cutting across and

5

Charles Russell read it.

'Hm,' he said at length. 'Pretty thin. Some student at the Massachusetts Institute works out a Do-it-Yourself nuclear weapon. It seems his professors believe it credible. They're going to do a radio programme, though naturally not stating the method.'

'You call that thin?'

'It is hardly precise. Something like this was in time inevitable. Making the Bomb is no longer a secret. It's a question of engineering resources.'

'Then it's come at a very awkward moment, an awkward moment for me, that is. And look who is taking an interest.'

'I have.'

The General got up to pour more brandy and while he did so Charles Russell reflected coolly. The organization the cutting had hinted at—it hadn't been named but was clearly suggested—roused various and wildly varying judgements. To some it was anathema, a secret defiance of constitutional government. Others went down on their knees and thanked God that in an age of universal shamming there still existed a hard core of *realpolitik*. His own view was somewhere between the two.

The General said quietly: 'That report has been published in other places besides the most sensible of your London newspapers. Naturally my masters have seen it.'

'They would hardly act on that alone.'

'You are right—they would not. But the fact that such a thing is possible makes my own position much more difficult. Call me "moderate" rather than "dove", if you please, but at bottom I'm a European.

6

Mass suicide is not to my fancy but I have masters who might conceivably risk it.'

'On a newspaper cutting?'

'No, not at all. But that cutting confirms that a nightmare is possible and my masters have frequent, persistent nightmares. So would you if you had suffered what we have.'

'Any evidence to support the nightmares?'

The General brought out another paper, reading a list of a dozen names. 'All these men are known to have gone to Germany,and some of those names you no doubt know. You won't deny me your opinion, between us, as to what degree of danger they offer.'

'They offer plenty of danger—murders and kid-nappings. But none has the brains for an organized framing.'

'Belami Clark,' the General said softly.

'Has he turned up in Germany too?'

'No, he's still in South America and causing our unnamed organization a good many understandable headaches.'

Charles Russell didn't answer at once. Belami Clark was heavy calibre, a man in a very much higher league. But he said at last: 'I still can't believe what you fear is on.'

'May I ask why not?'

'Then who puts up the money to work it?'

'Money?' the General asked. He looked puzzled. Charles Russell couldn't understand his puzzlement. The Executive had worked on a budget though of course there'd been devious ways around it, but if a plan of the Colonel-General's was passed the cash to finance it flowed at once. A simple question which to

Russell seemed natural had made the General stare and rub his chin. But he respected Charles Russell too deeply to doubt him. If Russell said lack of money could hinder then Charles Russell must be listened to carefully. So the General stroked his chin and suggested: 'That absurd little man in Northern Africa?'

'Possibly, but I rather doubt it. He keeps a very close rein on what he disburses; he's getting a bad name with the wild boys. You could call him a lender of last resort, and the conservative Arabs wouldn't touch it. Why should they? They'd be cutting their throats.'

'The man Belami Clark is currently working for?'

'Molina? Yes, in theory no doubt. He has an enormous fortune stacked in Switzerland but he also has plenty to cope with at home without dabbling in foreign adventures. Our American colleagues you once alluded to are making his seat as hot as they can.'

'In their shoes I'd do exactly the same.' The Colonel-General changed gear unexpectedly. 'I do wish you'd come in on this, Charles. That's the reason, as you'll have guessed, why I'm here.'

'You know very well I'm retired and enjoying it. What puzzles me, though, is why you want me. You say your hardliners are getting restive, and that I can perhaps understand; you say you fear some sort of frame-up, the biggest in the world's history so far since it wouldn't just frame a man or a group but the whole government of a prosperous state; you say wild men are collecting in Germany.' Charles Russell paused for a needed breath. 'Now if any of those things is true you'd be failing in your evident duty if you didn't have agents to smell them out.'

'Of course I have—we're not short of agents. One, a

woman, is very good indeed.'

Charles Russell made two guesses; stayed silent.

'But none of them really carries the guns if it came to a showdown among my masters. Naturally I show them this woman's reports and naturally they are read very carefully. But suppose she reported nothing to worry about, that the whole thing was a put-up job. I'd be asked for an assurance of that and so be in an impossible posture. Trying to prove a negative. Hopeless. However good this woman is she carries no political punch. But if I could say that *you* said All Clear I'd be stronger by many times and grateful. What I need is an ally of proven judgement, and if he happens to be a trusted enemy that, in a sense, makes my stand the stronger. You have the highest reputation, you know, and your interest is basically just like mine, to stop us all destroying ourselves. You have just the same motives to tell the truth and my masters, though jumpy, are far from fools. I'd believe what you said and so would they. I mean in these rather special circumstances.'

'I'm sorry,' Charles Russell said. 'I'm a has-been.'

The General began to pace the room. It was heavily furnished in the Victorian manner—huge leather armchairs and fine Persian carpets. It might have been almost any room in a rather old-fashioned London club except for a single academy picture hung in an ornate gilded frame. It was a view of the Kremlin, rather tastelessly done, with bright sunshine but a sprinkling of snow on those domes which even in life looked unreal.

The General at last sat down again. 'I regret your decision but I have to accept it. But there's another thing you could do—here in London. I believe you know James Campbell.'

'Not well. He belongs to my club and we sometimes chat. But he's a scientist and we've not much in common.'

'You could call him your first atomic physicist and he's also just come back from America. I could talk to our own top people of course——'

'But they won't know what James Campbell may. So if a chance occurs I will talk to Campbell, but only from my own curiosity. I can't undertake to report what he tells me.'

'I cannot ask that but I think he might interest you.'

'I doubt if he'll give much away.'

'Scientists are a peculiar race. Against the world outside they're as close as clams but among themselves they can chatter like women.'

'I'm the world outside.'

'But you're also Charles Russell.' The General smiled. 'You were kind to come.'

Charles Russell took his cue and rose. 'I've very much enjoyed this evening.'

The General saw Russell down to the car. 'You know how to contact me. Just in case.'

'Yes, I know how to contact a very old enemy.'

'I've a hunch that something is going to happen.'

Charles Russell, in the embassy car, had a similar hunch and he took it seriously. Less seriously the General's fear. Without Belami Clark to do the brain work, without money behind Mr Belami Clark, he believed that the General was over-reacting.

In this judgement of the situation Charles Russell was in principle right, but he had no way to know that across the Atlantic a counter-revolution was brewing which would ripen the plot which the General feared from suspicion of danger to present menace.

Two men sat in an elaborate room in the height of the Spanish rococo tradition. Molina and Belami Clark sat in silence, listening to the noise of the crowd as it seethed in the square outside the palace. It was the biggest of the palace's *salons*, a room for receptions and formal junketings, and Molina sat in a very grand chair which had overtones of a viceregal throne. Which in fact, years ago, it once had been. He was a wiry little man who moved gracefully, a *mestizo*, which in this country was rare. People of Spanish blood had guarded it and they still spoke the purest Spanish out of Spain. Nor had the natives desired to assimilate. They were proud and they nursed ancestral wrongs. Belami Clark respected them greatly, for a more recent sense of outrage drove him too.

He was sitting on another chair, less grand than Molina's but still imposing. Molina said as the crowd's roar rose: 'Why don't they *do* something?'

'*Who* do *what*?' Clark was this little dictator's man but he wasn't his servant, he wasn't subservient.

'The police, I meant.'

'The police do not dare.'

'The army, then?'

Clark laughed without the sound of amusement. 'The army hasn't been paid for three months.'

He retreated into silence, considering. The little man on the throne he must needs keep in with, but he'd made every mistake in the political book. He had risen to power by the orthodox road, on a network of cells and private strongarms, on blackmail and threats and often violence, on large promises of better times. And then, when the moment of crisis had fallen, he had taken over the country bloodlessly.

A copybook exercise, Clark thought sourly, but what had followed had been far from the book. Molina had made splendid promises and Molina now tried to keep them honourably. He let wages rise, he was soft with strikes. He disbanded his private corps of hard men, swearing he'd never permit a secret police. He even failed to purge the army—twenty-four generals, six thousand men. And all the officers were upper class. If Molina was any sort of Marxist, something which Belami Clark now doubted, he was really a very bad one indeed. He had turned out just another soft nationalist, the natural prey of the Power to the north.

The noise in the square outside increased again.

'What are they saying?'

'Give us bread.'

'There's no money for hand-outs. The loans have stopped.'

'The Americans have stopped them—yes. The others have followed suit like sheep. It's all part of a well considered plan.'

Molina said: 'You're still my adviser.'

'My advice is to run while we still have a chance to.'

'To Switzerland?'

'Where else than to Switzerland? You've a villa there and money to live on.'

Clark knew it was sixty million francs, over ten million English pounds. A numbered account in the city of Zurich had been offensive to the puritan Clark, much too typical of Latin corruption. Clark had disapproved austerely, refusing all aid and even advice, though he knew from thirty years' experience how these things were done by those who wished to. But now he was glad the fund existed. For Molina would be increasingly bitter, Molina wouldn't be close with his money. If Clark asked him for a million or two, for revenge, he would explain, though not fully, Molina would finance him happily.

Clark had very much bigger game in his sights than revenge on behalf of a fallen dictator. Everything he had done since Hiroshima, this work he'd accepted with foolish Molina, had been directed to his private end. Thirty years it had taken—too much time. But now he had the means at last, though not in the way he had planned. No matter. Sixty million Swiss francs. It was more than enough.

Molina was saying: 'You think we could make it?'

'I think we have a chance to make it.'

'How do we do it?'

Clark told him shortly.

Molina thought it over impassively. 'There seems to be more than one uncertainty.' He had a nicely developed sense of irony.

Belami Clark who had none whatever answered the remark at face value. 'Principally that your pilot has left you and I'm only a weekend flier myself. But there's one certainty on the other side. Within a matter of hours or maybe less that crowd outside will cease to be one. It will then become a mob—unpredictable. So it'll tear down this building stone by stone and nobody is going to stop it. You haven't a man who will try to stop it, far less any disciplined force to do so.'

Molina rose calmly. 'Then we'd better be going. Are you armed, my friend?'

'I am armed.'

'Just as well.'

They left through the magnificent doors, turning sharply right, then right again. Now they were in a corridor, and the farther it led from the state apartments the shabbier the corridor grew. At the end was an old iron door which Molina unlocked. Outside was a platform, a spiral staircase. Both men went down to ground level and looked around. Clark had never been here before. Few men had.

It was a curious scene, he found time to decide, reminiscent of the distant Orient rather than of a Catholic country. They were in a sort of compound or courtyard, the side they now stood on closed by a palace wall, the other three by modest cottages. There were three on each side and all nine were identical. They were in Molina's private harem. Clark remembered the Spanish world—*serrallo*. It wasn't pronounced with disapproval except in very religious circles; it was pronounced with laughter and real respect. After all this Molina was well past fifty. God grant that at his age I'm half as vigorous.

A third man joined them, saluting creditably. His uniform was clean and pressed and in his sword-frog he carried a sort of scimitar. Molina, officially solidly socialist, was in some ways a rather rigid traditionalist. Hence the scimitar with its eastern overtones, the guard who if he wasn't a eunuch was certainly an unfortunate man.

'*Buenas tardes, señor Presidente.*'

'*Buenas tardes, amigo.*' 'Comrade' had never quite caught on.

'The Greek lady, I imagine, sir.' The Greek lady was

the reigning favourite, which the guard considered perfectly natural. Greek women made the best whores by tradition.

'Why yes,' Molina said, 'the Greek.' He started to move but the keeper stopped him. The keeper began to shuffle his feet.

'What is it, man?' Molina was short. He was pressed for time but he didn't seem frightened.

'The password, *señor*. You know the rule.'

Molina had forgotten the password which was another little game with the past; he'd had other things to think about and in any case it changed every day. Another piece of elaborate orthodoxy. Molina wished he had never thought of it.

'You know who I am. To hell with the password.'

'But *señor,* you made me swear——'

'I unswear you now.'

'I cannot do it.' The harem keeper was an unfortunate man but he was also of pure Spanish blood. An oath was an oath and not to be trifled with.

'I cannot.' Incredibly his hand had fallen, down to the hilt of the monstrous sword.

Belami Clark shot the guard through the head.

Molina looked down at the fallen body. His face was suddenly almost pure *peon*, contempt and a bitter rage competing. But his voice was as calm and controlled as ever.

'You needn't have done that. Unnecessary.'

The oaf was holding us up. He was drawing his sword.'

'Which the wretched man didn't know how to use.' Molina frowned, still struggled with anger. 'At this moment we have no time to waste talking. The ethics of it I will discuss with you later.'

They went across the compound, walking fast, to the middle of the three opposite cottages. Here the noise of the crowd in the square was inaudible. Molina went in and looked around. No one was visible but a bath was running. Molina banged on the bathroom door with his fist.

'Come out of there and fast.'

'I'm naked.'

'Which I pay you to be on demand. Come at once.'

In fact she joined them wrapped in a bath towel. She was maybe thirty and far from stupid. Greeks had numerous defects but seldom that one, and she saw at once that something was wrong. Molina had never brought another man.

'The keys of your car, please.' He treated them generously.

She didn't demur. 'It's out at the back.'

'Then I'm borrowing it for a while. Wish me luck.'

As Clark started the engine Molina said: 'Hurdle number one and over it. Now for the airport and something much higher.'

They drove by back streets to the little airport. Just short of it Belami Clark stopped the car, puckering his eyes against the sun, staring at one of the smaller hangars.

'Your private plane is there all right.'

'So far so good. And the field looks deserted.'

Clark took another look. 'Not quite. No one is working, they're all in the square. But there are a couple of men in the tower. Flight Control.'

'Any men on the gate?'

'I'm pretty sure not.'

They drove to the hangar free of challenge and Clark

checked the little plane's controls. 'Plenty of petrol,' he said. 'We're lucky.'

'My pilot once said she's a bit of a bitch. You're sure you can fly this toy?'

'I can try.'

They started the engine and taxied out. There wasn't a soul to show an interest. Molina said: 'That's hurdle two.'

'I fear you forget something.'

'Why? Can't you fly her?'

'I'm learning to fly her—it isn't that. I was thinking of what's left of the army. This flight isn't cleared, you realize that, and after that snatch you gave special orders——'

'Very sensible orders too.' He was cool. 'Shoot anything down that isn't cleared. I wonder if anyone's there to do it.' If Molina felt any fear he concealed it.

. . . A failed dictator and all his own fault. But he isn't any sort of coward.

The aircraft had gathered speed by now and Belami Clark slid the stick back for take-off. When he had sufficient air speed he put down the starboard wing and turned east.

And a burst from a light A.A. gun missed behind them. One of the barrels was firing tracer and characteristically the shot drifted past them with a wholly deceptive air of laziness. Clark flew on steadily, gaining height. Another burst came up but also missed.

Molina asked: 'Out of range quite soon?'

'Of that one, yes, but you know there's another. Whether it's still manned I can't tell.'

His doubt was answered before he had finished by the unmistakable crack of a heavier weapon. The shell was well off target, burst harmlessly, but the next was rather better, below them. For a second the little plane shuddered, then seemed to rise. Clark caught her and Molina asked again: 'Are you all right?'

'I haven't been hit. I would guess that we've taken a splinter or two, but the controls still work and the engine is turning.'

'Till the next one comes.'

It came, a wide miss. A fourth and then a final silence.

'Pretty poor shooting,' Molina said casually.

'How otherwise should peasants shoot? Their officers left them days ago, paid, like your pilot, with American money. Now stop talking, please, while I pick up some landmarks.'

Molina obeyed the request at once. He had spoken of hurdles one and two, but he knew that the third was still before them and that that would be the highest of all. As the Old Sierra was also high, much too high for this little plane's maximum ceiling, it was impossible to fly over the top so they'd have to follow the railway through the pass. At its widest that was maybe a furlong and in other parts a good deal less. Moreover it was often in cloud. They hadn't instruments to navigate blind and Clark, at the best, was a competent amateur. Molina crossed himself heavily, then looked with a certain unease at Clark. If Clark had seen the gesture he'd think him scared. Which for the first time he had begun to be. And who wouldn't be? he excused himself reasonably. This was lunacy of the highest order. And yes, there was cloud above them. Hell.

Clark flew into it without a tremor. 'It may lighten above,' he said conversationally.

'And if it doesn't?'

'I'll take sixty to one. But I've picked up the shape of a peak I recognize. It's two miles to the south of the pass. We're correctly positioned.'

Unexpectedly Molina laughed. His forgivable moment of fear had passed and what he felt now was a simple excitement. Amusement too—it was genuinely funny. 'Correctly positioned' indeed! It was droll. Correctly positioned for something impossible, to fly through a hole in a wall they couldn't see. No sign of the railway below them whatever. They couldn't even see the Sierra.

Molina said without bravado: 'I've never been too much afraid of death but I'm terrified of any suffering.'

'You won't suffer, *amigo mío*—not at all. If I fly her into the rock there'll be nothing left. And incidentally I give it a minute. If we're alive in a minute we're on the right course. Two minutes after that and we're through.'

Molina unstrapped his watch. 'I'll start counting.'

Sixty seconds and nothing happened. Jesus.

'I thought I caught a glimpse of the railway.'

'Then you've better eyes than I have. Be quiet.'

The plane lurched suddenly, drunkenly sideways. Something was half seen, then gone. Belami Clark said: 'That was a close one.'

Molina was staying very quiet. He counted a hundred, then twenty more. Suddenly the cloud lifted. They were through.

And flying above a fertile plain, very different from Molina's stark country. In the distance, in the clear bright air, was a town of some size, a great river and an airport's outline. The fourth hurdle, this, but also the least of them.

'Will they let us land?'

'They can hardly refuse.'

'And after that?'

'That's up to you—it depends how you handle them. I doubt if they'll give us political asylum, and in any case that's not what we want. They'll bundle us out on the first flight available. Which is the Iberia flight to Spain this evening. Then on to Neuwald by the first connection.'

Neuwald and the villa in Switzerland. To the villa and sixty million francs. Clark had always known men he could use for his purpose, if not an organization in being then the potential for an organization, but he'd never had the money to meld them. Now he had both and he knew what to do with them. This failed dictator would set him up handsomely.

2

The jet liner droned on through the boring night to Madrid and later the villa at Neuwald, and Belami Clark, still tense and restless, guessed back at events as he thought they had happened. He would have done very well as a telly scriptwriter. For one thing he lacked all sense of humour and for another he thought in pictures, not in words.

What he saw was a room where he'd never been, not so different from Molina's *salon* because it too had been designed to impress before they had thought of making it comfortable. The shape of it was known the world over since it wasn't round and it wasn't square. It looked out on over-gardened lawns and the impression it aimed to give the visitor was one of a certain colonial grandeur, though of course without the slaves in the background. Two men had sat in it, both clearly strained. One man had been sitting behind the desk and a chunky man sat in an armchair and waited. He could afford to wait; he had the other as cold as mutton. In the distance a Marine Corps band was playing, practising for a ceremony that afternoon. It played 'Hail to the Chief', in the circumstances an impertinence.

The man behind the desk was running scared. The political skids were under him too. He looked like a small town general storekeeper but in fact he was very smart indeed. He had to be since he was here on a shoestring. He was frightened but he was also resentful, for what had he done that another hadn't? Except to be betrayed more disastrously. So the do-gooders and the bleeding hearts, the media and the Press had savaged him, just as they had that other but worse. He thought it very unfair indeed, and under pressure two of his creatures had talked, which was something in his world unthinkable, as unthinkable as it was in the Mafia.

The comparison he would not have admitted.

Nevertheless he was scared and anxious, for although the skids were under his feet he might just contrive to keep his balance till the storm, as he hoped, blew away in frustration. After all it wasn't the first time. No. Provided of course he did nothing of controversy, and what the chunky man was now demanding was controversial or it was nothing at all. 'We can't live with it any longer,' he said. 'Quite apart from our very special interest we can't have a pseudo-communist state in what's traditionally our own back yard.'

'You think Molina is really a communist?'

'Not in the sense he's a proper Marxist. He behaved like one at first—it suited his plans. But I doubt if he knows what the word really means. Molina is a randy *mestizo*—he'd be dead by now but for good Swiss *piquers*. How he keeps it up I can't imagine.' The voice held a hint of admiration, almost of naked masculine envy. The chunky man had once played pro baseball but all of three wives had quickly left him. None had had any trouble in court.

'Then who do you fear?'

'His adviser. Clark.'

'Is *he* a real communist, then?'

'*Much* more dangerous.'

It was curious, Chunky quietly reflected, that Clark's Christian name was seldom uttered, if indeed 'Christian name' was a term with meaning. It was certain he was no sort of Christian. Like many others in the world of Security Chunky had a fat file on Clark. Belami sounded vaguely French but Chunky hadn't a hint of evidence to support that Clark had French blood in his veins. On the contrary he seemed purely British. His grandfather had gone to Japan at some time around the turn of the century and Belami Clark was the third generation. They had traded and made a good deal of money, had been accepted quite soon as a part of the scenery, but they'd always gone home for their brides to breed from. Not that they'd shown the least inhibition at some of the pleasanter local customs. Clark's father had had a charming mistress and Clark himself three boys by another. He had had, that is, till the first Big Bang had destroyed them and his way of life. He himself had been absent on business. A pity.

A great pity as it had later turned out for he hadn't forgotten and never forgiven. Chunky, who liked things too simply tagged, had decided that he was psychopathic (a word he used much but could not have defined) in his passion against the West which had wronged him. Whatever your word he was known to be dangerous and now he was right hand to Molina. Whom he was probably using in some way not evident.

A very uncomfortable situation.

The man behind the desk blew his nose. It was a prominent organ and less than handsome, a cartoonist's delight which he tried to hide. Photographs must be full face or nothing. He was quoting what Chunky had said before: ' "We can't have a pseudo-communist state in what's traditionally our own back yard." But isn't all that a little old-fashioned?'

The chunky man said with a dangerous candour: 'That's for you to decide. I'm not in Congress.' He had little respect for politicians and for one living on borrowed time he had none. He was head of what was called an Agency and a very powerful man indeed.

The older man retreated at once, saying peaceably: 'Then run through it again.'

'For less provocation from a communist closer we slapped on a trade embargo at once.'

'The "we" was a different administration.'

'That's all water under the bridge in any case. What concerns us is that uranium ore. If they cut off that, and I guess they're going to, the Pentagon will howl like wolves and you know what a punch they pack in Congress. Both Houses at that, clear across the country. Lose that and you can count life in days. Your political life, I mean. Think it over.'

The man behind the desk took this angrily; he said in his grating Square State snarl, with an attempt at a rather feeble sarcasm: 'You want me to send the Marines in?'

'No. To use your own words that's a little old-fashioned. We could do it of course, it's the ultimate sanction, but it would stir up an international wasps' nest. We favour a palace revolution.'

'You could pull it?'

'I think so. Inflation is running at four hundred per cent, as much as it was in Chile, or more. Most people are fed to the teeth with Molina. And we've his brother here—in moth balls, for use. I opposed the

24

decision to give him asylum but now I am glad I was overruled. He's living in New Mexico on a pension from non-accountable funds. He will certainly do as he's asked. Or he'll starve.'

'Their army?' the other asked.

'Is a joke. It will follow the rising star in any case. It hasn't been paid for several months.'

The man behind the desk considered. 'And internationally?' he inquired at last.

'The usual bad feeling in liberal circles, which happily are totally impotent. Great Britain will accept refugees since she still takes a pride in being cheated. One or two others will cancel football matches. The one Power which could intervene with effect will rumble but in the event do nothing. Molina's country is too far away. That lesson was learnt over Cuba finally.'

The band was still playing 'Hail to the Chief' and for the first time the man in Clark's picture heard it. Something like ribald laughter had shaken him; he had wiped his eyes, then had spat in his handkerchief. 'Okay,' he had said, 'go ahead and chance it. But try to keep my nose clean, will you?'

These images had been notably accurate, but Charles Russell had had no need of images when he'd considered the Colonel-General's worries. In this he had been helped by chance for he had met James Campbell in the bar of his club. He wasn't a very social man and he was standing alone and a little forlorn. Charles Russell had nodded and offered a drink.

'That's really very kind indeed. If this club has a fault it's a trifle cliquey and I've been out of the country for over a year.' Austere and a bit of a natural loner tonight he was feeling the need of company. 'I've just come back from the States,' he said.

'I gather from Massachusetts.'

'That is so.' James Campbell looked at Russell sharply. 'You're still interested in my movements?' he asked. His manner had hardened from casual friendliness into something very close to suspicion.

'No, not at all—I'm a gent of leisure. But what I still do is to read the papers. And where you've just come from has been in the news.'

Unexpectedly James Campbell laughed. 'Come and have dinner,' he said. 'I'll explain.'

They made a notably disparate pair in that solid and somewhat conventional club, James Campbell thick-set and dark and saturnine, showing the unmistakable blood of the Black Douglas who had been his mother, Charles Russell tall and erect and worldly, casually dressed but carelessly elegant. They were on easy terms but not familiar, for they had worked together once before. The affair of that troublesome Pole, Russell thought. He had advised he was no sort of refugee, but the bleeding hearts had been influential and the Home Secretary had overriden Charles Russell. His constituency held many ex-Poles. But when this spy had discovered too much he had died. Unpleasantly as it had happened—very. James Campbell had contrived the accident.

So Campbell explained over dinner admirably, not talking down to a stupid non-physicist but chatting easily to an intelligent layman. It appeared there'd been somewhat alarming articles about a student who'd stumbled on something new. As journalism they were no doubt interesting but their readers must read with a certain scepticism. A breakthrough in engineering was one thing but in basic physics quite another, and no method had so far been discovered, and in Campbell's opinion never would be, of making the Bomb in a housewife's kitchen. The plain facts of science were rudely against it. For to make any sort of nuclear weapon one had first to lay hands on a single essential, known in the business, though maybe pompously, as weapon-grade fissionable material. In practice that usually meant plutonium.

Charles Russell had nodded. So far he'd been within his depth.

And plutonium was derived from uranium, mostly its isotope 238, and to produce enriched uranium, another word for its deadly isotope, you needed an enormous plant, either a diffusion plant or possibly a high-speed centrifuge. The cost of either was astronomical, say the price of one or of one and a half completely armed and equipped Polarises. Not a matter which smaller states could contemplate, even if they could lay hands on uranium which nowadays was increasingly policed.

Then how was it that Israel and India . . .?

Ah, that brought in a different factor, the question of nuclear power, not the Bomb. All industrial states must somehow develop it or stay hostages to Arab blackmail, and in any case oil was like anything else; it was finite and wouldn't last for ever. So the Indian case was an illustration. Some years ago the trusting Canadians had sold them a research reactor under conditions at that time thought more than adequate but which later developments had shown to be futile. For even the smallest research reactor meant some quantity of the vital plutonium and a modern reactor bred plutonium freely. So a bang in the desert of Rajasthan. The

Canadians had been somewhat ingenuous, but to do those wretched Indians justice, something James Campbell found hard to do, he didn't believe they had made a Bomb. There was an exception to every rule made by man and he thought that for once they were telling the truth when they prated about peaceful uses. And as for Israel he didn't know, but if they hadn't actually made the Bomb they could do so at very short notice indeed. Down in the Negev, a desert again, there was a formidable, closely guarded establishment.

Charles Russell finished his plate and considered. Not all of what Campbell had told him was new to him, and clearly none of this was classified. James Campbell was no idle talker, simply a man who was good at exegesis. Charles Russell decided he'd probe a bit further.

'There's a Non-Proliferation Treaty and an Agency which sits in Vienna. No doubt it does whatever it can, particularly over supplies of uranium, but if I'm understanding you rightly what counts is plutonium, and any programme for atomic energy means plutonium is produced as well.'

'That puts it very succinctly and I can guess what a man like you is thinking. Somebody hijacks a load of plutonium . . .' James Campbell shrugged. 'I can't deny it's on in theory—any hijacking is on in theory—but I don't believe it's on in practice. Unscrupulous states may play dangerous games, indeed we've been talking of cases in point, but for criminals to lay hands on plutonium would be a coup of an order so far unachieved. All countries are aware of the risks. And plutonium is radioactive, so to steal it from a nuclear power station would need a body of skilled and protected scientists who would also need to be highly trained infantrymen. The combination is somewhat uncommon. And when it is moved the precautions are serious, much more serious than moving gold. No half measures with some private security firm.'

'You comfort me,' Charles Russell said. He reflected again, then moved a step further. 'You think any hijack just isn't on?'

'I told you I don't think it's on in practice.'

'A friend of mine has a different worry. He doesn't fear making a Bomb in secret; he fears the appearance that that might be happening.'

'I don't think I follow.'

'I didn't myself at first. I do now. If Germany tried to make the Bomb——'

'Germany is far too sensible.'

'But if the belief were somehow built up that she was——'

'Russia would act within twenty-four hours.'

'Precisely,' Russell said. 'Precisely. Though not every Russian's a screaming hawk.' He pushed his plate aside. 'Some cheese?'

Campbell said: 'Damn the cheese.' He was hooked. His naturally saturnine face had frozen in lines of something near horror. 'What are you trying to tell me? Come clean.'

'I've come perfectly clean, I know no more. But I've a friend, and he's a moderate man, who is frightened of an organized plan to persuade his masters that Germany's cheating.' Charles Russell had ordered black coffee and brandy; he sipped the former and sniffed at the latter. 'Now tell me, do you think that possible—to build up that belief, I mean, to a point where hardheaded men would take action?'

'Germany,' James Campbell said thoughtfully. He ignored his own coffee but drank his brandy; he signalled to the wine waiter quietly. 'The same again, please. I need it badly.

'Germany,' he said again. 'You've chosen a rather special case. Germany has a very real head start in the European race for atomic power. We boast that we produce more than most but the Magnoxes are out of date and the second generation failures. To catch up in a very hard-run race we have either to buy what America offers which in my opinion we should, though they're tricky, or else build our own which we don't seem too good at. That's a matter of internal politics and I try to keep out of those at all costs. But the Germans haven't concentrated on immediate returns from functioning stations. They bought themselves into the second sons and are raising the third generation successfully. No physicist really likes the words but "fast breeders" is the popular term.'

'All busy breeding plutonium?'

'There's plenty of that in the Federal Republic.'

'A background for my friend's fear?'

'I suppose so.'

'You don't sound too convinced.'

'I am not. But then I didn't lose six million men or have the best part of my country ravished.'

They paid their bills at the desk and went downstairs. The porter found James Campbell a taxi but Russell decided to walk for the exercise.

And as he turned into his quiet street in doctorland a big black saloon was outside his flat. There was a man at the wheel, bolt upright and vigilant, and two others on the pavement, watching. They wore foreign-looking overcoats and were staring down the street, one each way. As Russell passed the first he shifted his feet. 'Good evening,' Russell said. The guard said nothing.

As Russell reached the car the door opened. A man got out quickly and flicked at his hat. It was more than a gesture of recognition, rather less than a parade ground salute. The General said: 'I am being a nuisance.'

'It *is* a little late, perhaps.'

'I have a flight to catch in an hour and a half. I'd be greatly obliged if——'

'Then please come in.'

They went up to Russell's flat and he stood aside. The General went in and Russell followed him. 'Brandy?' he inquired.

'I thank you.'

'It isn't your own.'

'It is just as good.' In fact it was a great deal better.

The General drank most of his glass, then sat down. 'I wouldn't have disturbed your evening if something very serious hadn't happened. You've read the evening paper?'

'No. But I looked at the ticker down at my club.'

'Then you know that Molina's government has fallen.'

'Also I can guess who fixed it.'

'They were doing their duty,' the General said. He wasn't a man to bear resentment because other professionals had other objectives. 'But what isn't generally known just yet, what I very much doubt if the ticker told you, is that both of them got clean away.'

'You mean Molina and Belami Clark?'

'I do. They've gone to a place called Neuwald in Switzerland.'

'Where Molina has stacked an illicit fortune. What more natural place to choose to enjoy it? And in any case they've not gone to Germany.'

'Neuwald's just across the lake. There's a regular ferry connecting two roads.'

'Aren't you jumping to conclusions a little?'

'I'm jumping to no conclusions yet, simply telling you facts which I do not like. Here's Clark who we agreed is dangerous within a ferry ride of Western Germany. Here's Molina with a great deal of money. The combination has a clear potential.'

'You think Molina might stake up Clark?'

'I don't see why he shouldn't do that. Molina will be resentful and sore. If Clark puts up any sort of scheme which Molina thinks is anti-American Molina will conceivably back it without asking questions about what more is involved. An angry man soon loses his judgement.'

'You have a point,' Charles Russell said.

'In that case I repeat my request. I'd like you to go to Neuwald and report.'

'I can only say what I told you before. I'm retired,' Charles Russell said, 'for good.'

The General permitted a sceptical smile. 'But if I'm rightly informed and I mostly am you've had various, let us call them adventures, since a retirement which I for one regretted.'

'Not in this class, I haven't. No indeed. And in any case you told me yourself you had a perfectly competent agent on the job. A woman, I think you said, so I made two guesses.'

'One was almost certainly right. The lady's name is Helen Monteath.'

32

'I can think of no more attractive bait but the fact remains she is working for you and I don't care to bend the rules in retirement.'

'Then the answer is no still?'

'It is. With regret.'

3

Molina and with him Belami Clark had arrived at Molina's imposing villa but the journey hadn't been wholly smooth. Their neighbour across the Old Sierra had allowed them to land as Clark had said she would and had bundled them onto the flight for Madrid with an indulgence which had been mixed with alarm. To let them stay for longer than hours in a country which in effect was a satellite might embarrass her with the Power to the north on which she depended for basic existence.

But in Madrid it hadn't been quite so easy, less a matter of any open hostility than a typically Spanish passion for protocol . . . . So they had landed without their passports? A frown. Señor Molina was an eminent person and Mr Clark was no doubt within his protection so what was an impropriety could be overlooked as a special case. But the gentlemen wished to fly on to Zurich? Ah, that raised rather different problems. For one thing the Swiss were extremely punctilious, and for another it would break Spanish law to let a man cross her frontiers paperless, without something to show at least his identity. The senior official's voice had hardened. The Señor's country had an embassy here whose business it was to assist its subjects, but in the rather special circumstances the Señor might not wish to avail himself of the services which that embassy offered. That was so? Understandable but also a pity.

For then it might take weeks in formalities before some travel document could be drafted and issued.

Molina had handled the impasse perfectly. He'd been carrying a large sum of money—he'd been doing this now for several months—but the Spanish half of his blood was pure Spanish, so he didn't flash his roll like a tourist or directly refer to the matter of money. Instead he simply said he was sorry that already overworked officials should be burdened with further avoidable duties for which he was the reluctant cause. It was a kindness which he would never forget. And might he ask a further favour, the chartering of an aircraft to Zurich? In passing, the arrangements for that would present no sort of financial difficulty. No bill need be sent to Molina's embassy. Embassies were much slower than people when it came to settling debts of honour.

The documents arrived next morning and the aircraft took off on time at three. At Zurich there'd been a car at the airport and the villa had been Swiss-clean, the staff smiling. Molina was an excellent master.

Molina went straight to bed and slept. He had a formidable resilience and could sleep like a baby whenever he chose, but Clark was much too tense for sleep. He smoked a cigar but he did not drink. He did not drink on principle, believing it blunted his dedication. So he sat in the dark, on edge but contented. For he could see the end of his road at last.

It hadn't been an easy one, thirty years of it—that was too much time. He'd been anywhere where an American interest existed and could therefore be damaged. Korea at first and later Vietnam, the Congo and finally missions in Israel for Arabs whom he'd learnt to despise. And always the vision fading backwards. A single man, however dedicated, could do little against a powerful state. Annoy it perhaps, make its Agencies watch him, even make it worth while to plot his murder. There'd been two attempts at this, both failures. Annoyances then, even minor setbacks on the frontiers of the American empire. But Clark hadn't committed his life to annoyances. He wanted to see America burning as America had burnt his children.

With hundreds of thousands of others. His way of life.

He'd been twenty-five when this had happened and now he was fifty-five and ageing. He turned on a light and walked to a mirror. The face of an ascetic priest looked back at him with severe disapproval.

As he today disapproved of Molina, for Molina had been the worst of his let-downs. He had heard of him when he'd been working in Israel, once almost betrayed by Arab incompetence, once almost betrayed by Arab malice. He had sounded like the Grail at last for Molina had revolted successfully against the stifling embrace of the country Clark hated. In his wanderings Clark had made useful contacts and soon Molina had asked him to join him. He had needed a man of wide experience, an adviser to explain the policies of countries to which he had never been. His own diplomats he quite rightly mistrusted and his entourage was like himself, men of a limited education who knew little of the outside world.

And Molina had let Clark down with a bang. Clark had thought he was some sort of Marxist, a religion which Clark had never adopted since in the last resort it wouldn't serve him, it wouldn't risk a global showdown unless it could be tricked into doing so. And Molina had been no sort of anarchist, a word which Clark, when he thought in words, would not have rejected out of hand. The chunky man in the oval room had, not for the first time, got it wrong. Molina wasn't even the pseudo-communist which the chunky man had once suggested, simply a man who'd contrived a victory in a long line of Latin American coups. And he hadn't the very slightest intention of cutting off his uranium ore. What he was doing was putting the price up—up and up and up again. There was precedent for that elsewhere, and when the rumblings turned into open threats he would brake the blackmail for maybe a year. Then on would go the pressure again. They had to have the stuff at any price or the balance of terror would soon cease to have meaning.

He'd miscalculated by exactly one rise.

Belami Clark had begun to despise him but he couldn't cast the man aside. He had a very good reason not to do that, or rather sixty million reasons. He was tied to this little *mestizo* helplessly.

Who summoned him next morning early. He was eating his breakfast in bed, scrambled eggs, but his manner was one Clark had never seen. He didn't offer a chair but left Clark standing. Clark, who wasn't normally subservient, said with an unusual formality:

'Good morning, Excellency.'

Molina ignored it. 'That man,' he said crisply.

'Which man?'

'My guard. The one you shot down without my orders.'

Belami Clark was entirely astonished. He had heard Molina say he'd discuss it but he'd taken this as a form of words, a saving of face for distasteful action which in fact would never be mentioned again. Clearly he had been very wrong so he stood there silent and watched Molina.

'Have you anything to excuse yourself?'

'What I told you before which I think is enough. We were pressed for time and the man was hindering.'

'Did you not hear me call him *amigo*?'

'*Amigo* is a word like another.'

Molina was suddenly bitterly angry, his face set again in the sharp lines of a *peon*'s. 'It is no such thing, it is not like "comrade". When I call a man friend he *is* my friend. Whom you shot before my eyes without orders. If I were in my country still I would put you before a court for judgement.'

Clark wisely didn't answer this. For one thing he was still too surprised and for another he didn't have an answer.

When Molina had cooled a little he said: 'On the other hand I owe you my life. If you hadn't flown me out I'd be dead. You may stay here or go as you please. But choose now.'

'I'd like to stay,' Clark said at last.

'Very well. But in turn I'd prefer not to see you for a while. Say ten days or a fortnight. Take a car—go away. When you come back I can hope to forgive you.'

Clark went to his room and packed his bag. He would think out this new situation later, this astonishing man in the bed he had never met, but for the moment it wasn't totally loss. It would now be unexpectedly difficult to part this new stranger from large sums of money, but equally he'd been given reason for absence which he badly needed. For he had urgent work to do in Germany.

He chose the Mercedes which turned out well, for it

got him across the German frontier. At the Swiss there was no trouble whatever since the control post had been warned in advance of two *laissez passers* held by foreigners which were to be honoured until a time came to cancel them. They let him drive to the ferry which crossed the lake.

But on the German side of the lake it was different. This post was manned by quite minor officials and the document which Clark now carried was something which none had ever seen. . . . Was he Spanish, then? He was certainly not. Was the car his own? He produced its log book; he had carefully checked it before taking the vehicle. A muttered conversation in German, then the question which was intended as killer. Money—had he adequate funds? Clark produced more than adequate funds, his savings from seven months' work with Molina who had paid him, as he always paid, generously. Clark had changed it to marks before leaving for Germany.

The atmosphere changed in turn at once from suspicion to something quite close to fear. Clark thought it all distastefully German, a people, he had heard it said, who were either at your throat or at your knees. Be that as it might the money clinched it. Here was a man with a large German car, with more money than all of them earned in a year. If they let him through on the sort of paper which they'd none of them ever seen before there was a risk they were making some sort of mistake, but if they held this clearly affluent man and he was really the bigwig he seemed to be the results could be tough for junior officials. As good Germans they took the lesser risk.

Clark drove off the ferry and up to Ulm. He had

already arranged for his contacts to meet him there. He hadn't the funds to finance them finally till he'd persuaded Molina to part with real money, but he had something like ninety thousand marks which he'd honestly earned by his curious lights and were undoubtedly his private property. But Belami Clark had no feeling for money: it was simply a means to an end, his last one. These ninety thousand hard-earned marks would serve until he laid hands on more. It would serve to keep his contacts going and with them the first step in his plan.

He drove to a quiet hotel and slept, and next morning the first of these contacts met him. His list would have intrigued the General since in substance it was almost identical. But it was also several names the shorter. Clark had no time whatever for Arabs who twice had nearly cost him his life. So this list would have intrigued the General but it would also have done the same to Russell, who took a more than academic interest in men who would destroy their world in order to start it again in innocence. Three were Spanish in the classic tradition: anarcho-syndicalism had been a force there for centuries. One was a Belgian and another was, of all things, Dutch. Two more were Japanese—the best. Belami Clark spoke their language fluently. One was an Englishman. Clark frowned uncertainly. Englishmen had some curious values and he was the only man in the list Clark didn't know.

And all of them had come to Germany for the reason Charles Russell had given the General. They were interested in mischief generally, any outrage against the system they hated, and Germany was the softest target, much softer than France or even Italy. Belami Clark didn't feel quite one of them—his objective was well defined, theirs were misty—but at least they had what he had himself, a sort of committed desperation. All terrorists must have that to operate. Unlike the Arabs, now omitted, all were and always had been loners. So much the better, Clark thought; he would meld them; he would give them a clear purpose at last.

He left Ulm after seventeen days, delayed, for there'd been a mishap which he'd had to attend to. All eight men had accepted his leadership since all of them knew his reputation, but one of them had changed his mind. The Englishman had come back in a couple of days, insisting that the scheme was a lunacy. The risks were too great, the uncertainties legion. Clark hadn't argued, he'd let him go. But he had known what he must do and do quickly. This man had been told too much; he was dangerous.

It had taken three extra days to arrange his death. Clark killed him himself without anger or mercy. What was a single human life against the background of Hiroshima's outrage?

He returned by the same route to Neuwald, presenting himself to Molina confidently. Molina had made him a promise in terms—you can go or stay and he'd chosen to stay. Molina wouldn't break a promise.

Nor did he but he received Clark cooly. 'Nice holiday?' he inquired.

'I enjoyed it.'

'Then we'll have dinner tonight and discuss your travels. Just at the moment I've another engagement.' Clark didn't ask him what it was but Molina volunteered it happily. 'I intend to go down to the Bleiner hotel. I've been here for over a fortnight. Alone.'

'Good hunting,' Clark said.

'Thank you. I need it.'

Belami Clark had understood him. Molina had been in Neuwald a fortnight, a fortnight without a woman. Unprecedented. So he'd go down to the Bleiner and talk to the porter; he'd give him an outrageous tip. Even in this bourgeois town the porter of a hotel like the Bleiner would know where to find what Molina wanted.

Molina skipped the casual dinner date and Belami Clark went to bed at eleven.

And in the small hours he woke with the Terror upon him. It had dogged him since the event itself, thirty years of an inescapable nightmare, coming often at first and later less frequently, but it had never lost its power to shatter him. His mind which by habit worked in pictures in a nightmare added an extra horror.

He had been returning from a business trip, eager to meet his Japanese mistress and the three children she had gladly borne him. It had been a successful trip and Clark had been happy. He loved this life and he loved his family. Later, he supposed, he must marry, returning home for a bride who would probably bore him as his mother had bored his father to death. But that would come later, quite a bit later, and he didn't propose to think of it now. He was twenty-five, quite well off and fulfilled. He spoke Japanese just as well as English, he was the third generation, almost wholly assimilated, and though they made him report once a week to the police, though he knew he was discreetly watched, he hadn't been interfered with openly.

The train had been running through open country, perhaps a mile from the busy town and his home. When the first of the great winds came it fell over. It fell on the side away from Clark, its momentum forcing it on for a while, what was wood in the carriage splintering savagely, the steelwork screaming along the track. For an instant there was almost silence, then the clamour of Orientals in panic. Clark had heard it once in his life before when a ferry between two islands had foundered. He had hoped he would never hear it again.

When he had himself in hand he scrambled out, sliding down the free side of the carriage. Behind him was an insensate uproar, human beings reduced to the level of animals, in front of him where his city had been. Unbelievably it wasn't there. In its place was a mushroom-shaped pall of smoke.

Belami Clark began to run, down the road which ran alongside the railway. He knew nothing of bombs or of radio-activity, nothing of the dreadful dangers. He was twenty-five and a man with a family. Something wholly appalling had happened and he ran towards them blindly, praying.

Soon the first of the panic exodus caught him, the people from outer suburbs, these, with cars which could run still or sometimes horses. They drove him from the road without mercy, screaming words which he considered meaningless. . . . The end of the world, a volcano, an earthquake. And always the unrelenting *leitmotif*. There was fire, there was fire, the fires of hell.

He took refuge in the ditch at last as the short-lived torrent of traffic engulfed him. It swept by him for perhaps ten minutes, then, as suddenly as it had come, was gone. Clark shakily crawled from the dirty ditch.

He wished he had not; all his life he wished that. For two furlongs behind the spurt of traffic came the first of the walking survivors. He shuddered. Men staggering, supporting each other, half naked, their clothes in torn and blackened rags. Women with frozen faces and sometimes stoically carrying dead children.

Belami Clark went back to the ditch. He had a weapon and he intended to use it. When he felt he could manage to shoot himself cleanly.

It was thus that the four Swedes found him, hysterical. They were the last of an outlying hospital staff and they had stayed till they knew it was finally hopeless. A woman in the back tapped the driver.

'There's a man in that ditch. A European.'

The driver said: 'Leave him.' He meant just 'Leave him'. He was a doctor not a scientist but he'd been reading his country's well informed newspapers and he had guessed that something appalling was brewing; he had guessed at the spreading menace behind his car. What was chasing it was simply death, an invisible lingering miserable death.

The woman had seemed to be in charge. 'Nonsense,' she'd said briskly. 'Get him.'

'He seems to be armed.'

'Then take it away.'

The driver hesitated but got down from the car. Belami Clark said: 'No,' and raised the gun. The Swede, very neatly, kicked it away. With his other foot he kicked Belami's jaw. Then he lifted him across his shoulders and carried him back to the hospital car. The two women in the back were silent. The driver threw Clark across their knees. 'Your patient,' he said, 'and I hope not contaminated.'

Belami Clark woke shaken and sweating, the Black Dog still riding his shoulders in consciousness. It hadn't snarled at him for several years but it still had the power to lay him prostrate.

He got up and showered and changed his pyjamas. Then he lay down again but not to sleep, letting his bitter commitment engulf him. Men capable of such an outrage, a civilization (they called it that) which had even dared consider it, had earned only one fate and that was destruction. But a single man could never encompass it—thirty years of disappointment had taught him that. He could often embarrass and sometimes frustrate, but only in pinpricks, mere trifles to a major Power. The only way to bring it to justice was to trap it into destroying itself.

He believed he was now within distance of doing it.

A rare flash of unaccustomed irony split his face in a vicious death's-head grin. He saw Her, as always, in vivid pictures, not Justice with her sword and scales but Justice with the fool's striped bladder.

A little before dawn he dropped off, waking in peace again, almost contented. He even began to count his blessings, deciding he'd had his share of good fortune. Molina had bought a villa in Switzerland for the reason his shameful fortune was hidden there, but he needn't have chosen Neuwald to settle. He had done so because his doctor lived there, a remarkable man with a remarkable practice, and also for his second hobby which he pursued with an almost equal passion. This was waterskiing and the ugly lake suited it. It was either so rough that the sport was impossible or else it was perfectly, glassily calm, far better than any southern sea. And across it was the Federal Republic, the priming charge for the final explosion.

And one other blessing, he thought unsmiling.

45

Neuwald held a great laboratory, Lenterheims, apparently Swiss.

At nine o'clock he sent up a message that if Molina could spare him a minute he'd like to see him. Molina was eating breakfast again, his manner what it had been the day before. It wasn't hostile but nor was it friendly. Clark had assumed that a night with a woman would have mellowed him into a certain ease, but in this he had made a miscalculation. For the woman the Bleiner's porter had found him had been German-Swiss and extremely dull. Molina had paid her what she had asked for but had withheld his usual generous present. He'd regretted the evening as a waste of time, more importantly as a waste of resources. 'Sit down,' he said. 'What is it? Tell me.'

Clark began to do so succinctly, watching Molina's expression closely. But he had put on his *peon*'s face at once, graven in deep lines and inscrutable. This was the first move in Clark's grand plan and for it he needed a great deal of money. So he told it as he had planned to tell it, not lying—Molina was much too shrewd—but concealing what was his final intention from a man who would almost certainly shy from it.

Molina had sat propped up on cushions, stroking the bitch which had jumped on the bed. She stared at him with hunt terrier's pop eyes, adoring, in her private heaven. Clark thought the dog a very bad omen. When he'd left for his busy trip to Germany Molina hadn't owned a dog. Dogs were a symptom of self-indulgence, of a weakening will to face reality.

But he said nothing of this to the man on the bed; he went on to the end and then summarized shortly. 'That's the plan,' he said. 'I can bring it off. But of

46

course I shall need the money to do it.'

Molina didn't answer at once and Clark had an increasing impression that for the second time he'd misjudged Molina. He had gone to his country because it looked promising, the classic South American set-up of a patriot trying to break the bonds which bound it to a too-powerful neighbour. Had Molina really intended that? The too-powerful neighbour had certainly thought so since it had contrived and financed a revolution, but Clark had begun to have more than one doubt. He could just forgive the numbered account since one couldn't change a leopard's spots which in the case of most Latins were normally gold ones, but Molina had shown little sign of resentment and none whatever of furious anger. On the contrary he seemed to be perfectly happy, to be settling to life in Neuwald contentedly.

Which was going to present a difficulty which Clark had not foreseen or imagined. Molina was going to be hard to touch.

He said at last: 'I'm not sure I follow. How would kidnapping a nuclear scientist in any way advance my interests?'

'This scientist is rather a special one. He's just come back from America, from a place where there've been most secret developments.'

Molina didn't query this statement. He knew he was an ignoramus in most worldly affairs outside his country and he'd hired Belami Clark to keep him informed of them. But closer to home he was sharp as a razor; he wouldn't have come to the top if he hadn't been.

'We could use him as political blackmail?'

'*You* could,' Clark said. 'You're the politician.'

Again it wasn't a lie directly, though Clark hadn't much faith in political leverage, and in restoring Molina to power in his country Clark had no interest of any kind. His interests were suspicion and fear. Build those with skill and relentless pressure and you'd be something more than half-way home. So snatch a well-known nuclear scientist and the Security men of half the world would be biting their nails and demanding instructions. That was only a start but would set the scene. Later developments, merely suspicious, would soon become something more—they'd be sinister. Sinister enough and frightening enough, enough of them and well enough timed. . . .

Somebody would lose his head. Politicians always did in the pinches.

Molina had been thinking silently. At length he said: 'You mentioned money.'

'A good deal, I'm afraid.'

'How much?'

'Two million.'

The man on the bed said nothing at all; he stroked the terrier and she stared back at him blissfully. His face was still South American Indian, dignified, grave and entirely expressionless. 'Francs?' he inquired at last.

'I meant pounds.'

For a full minute Molina didn't answer but when he did so his voice was quietly final. 'I told you before, I owe you my life. That I do not forget and I never shall. I think your scheme an uncertain one and I suspect you haven't told me everything. Do you mean to hide this man in my house?'

'If you permit it.'

Molina considered this impassively. He was prepared

to take a limited risk in the hope of some possible future advantage. 'I'll permit it on two express conditions: the first is that one week is the limit and the second that neither I nor my servants be in any way involved in his presence. Two of them are, as you know, my bodyguards, but if you need another to watch this scientist him you must provide yourself.'

'That I can do,' Clark said and he meant it. The Dutchman he thought—he would do the job admirably. He had all of his race's tedious defects, he asked too many boring and awkward questions, but he was obedient and entirely reliable and he spoke German which Belami Clark did not. If anything went wrong he'd be safe. For an instant Clark felt a twinge of sympathy for any policeman who tried to break this Dutchman. Moreover he had a specialized skill and had done time as a perfectly ordinary criminal. At the moment Clark knew of no use for this skill, but one could never be sure. It could still come in handy.

Molina said with a crisp authority: 'I wish to make my position quite clear. I'm beginning to like this life in Neuwald and I intend to lead it out unmolested, at any rate till I decide on another. If there's a chance to return to my country I'll take it, but I don't think I'd care to put that higher. Now returning to the matter of money, I think you said two million pounds.'

'I'll need all of that if I'm going to help you.'

Talking to Charles Russell in London the General had feared that Molina might jump at it. . . . 'An angry man soon loses his judgement.' But in this he had misjudged Molina who however resentful at losing his country had a very sharp sense of the value of money.

'Help me?' he asked now. 'To return? But I consider

49

that aspect a little obscure. Even if you pull off this kidnap I don't yet see how I'm going to use it. But if you need money I owe you that.' He reached to a bedside table and wrote a cheque. 'And your salary will of course continue till you do anything to cause me to stop it.' He handed the cheque to Clark who took it.

. . . Two hundred thousand pounds, a paltry tenth. He doesn't believe a word I'm saying, he's simply trying to pay me off, the fine gentleman he believes he is.

Belami Clark went back to his room. The interview had depressed him severely for Molina hadn't behaved as expected. Far from burning for revenge and a comeback he'd been cool on the second, ignored the first. Clark decided what he'd begun to suspect. Molina was rotten all through, a degenerate, just another little Latin dictator who had robbed the country he'd pretended to serve and now had his eyes on the fleshpots firmly.

In this he was disastrously wrong, but that lay in the future, he couldn't foresee it. He looked at the cheque again and almost smiled. Two hundred thousand pounds—a *douceur*. But it was enough for the moment, enough to start with. Later he'd have to think again.

He packed a bag and flew to London where he contacted one of the two Japanese whom he'd already dispatched to await his arrival.

James Campbell remembered little about it for it had been very well organized and carried out expertly. There'd been a ring at his door in the night and a well spoken voice. 'I'm the doctor,' it said, 'and I've brought an ambulance.'

Campbell realized at once that there'd been a

mistake. These flats housed several elderly people and perhaps one of them upstairs was in trouble. In which case he would give directions. He opened the door, quite unsuspecting.

Two men stood on his doorstep wearing white. One was a European, the other appeared to be Japanese, and both had an air of professional urgency. The European asked briskly: 'Where's the casualty?'

'Not here, I'm afraid. There's some mistake. But if you'd give me the name I could maybe help.'

'A mistake?' the doctor asked. He frowned. He seemed to have a very slow mind. 'May we come in for a moment?'

'Of course.'

Campbell stood aside politely but the Japanese managed to stumble against him. He felt a sudden sharp stab in his arm through his dressing-gown. There was a moment of dizziness. Then he fell down.

After that he remembered only the outlines. He was conscious though he couldn't cry out or move but he could see through an increasing blur. . . . The ambulance in the street outside, getting out a stretcher, rolling him in. What appeared to be a disused airfield, pulling him into an aircraft and strapping him in. Then the landing and another car, an interminable drive with the blinds pulled down. He'd had the impression that they'd crossed a frontier for there'd been foreign voices but English speech. Belami Clark had been talking them over. . . . A very sick man and a very rich one going home with a doctor and male nurse to die. To Neuwald where this tycoon had been born. Clark knew the Swiss and 'rich man' would do it. The forged passports had cost much money, were good ones.

Nobody looked inside the car.

And nobody showed any interest at Neuwald. At Molina's villa large cars were common and if they arrived with the blinds pulled down that was the business of wealthy Molina. Riches, great wealth—one was reared to respect them. The last thing one did was to ask them questions.

When Campbell recovered normal consciousness a man was bending over his bed. He was the doctor but no longer in white. He examined James Campbell and rang a bell. He said to the Japanese who answered it:

'He's conscious again or almost conscious. Give him another shot but not the same.'

4

The first news that Charles Russell had that James Campbell had mysteriously vanished was given him in the bar of his club. He didn't know the man very well but he knew he was a colleague of Campbell's. He sat down beside Russell and said softly but urgently: 'Could I have a word with you, sir?'

Russell looked at him: this was clearly not social. 'In another room?' he suggested.

'Yes please.'

They went into the little used card room and the other man came to the point at once. 'James Campbell has disappeared,' he said.

Russell didn't answer; he waited.

'He didn't turn up on Wednesday morning, so we rang his flat and there wasn't an answer. We didn't take that too seriously since there were a dozen things he might have been doing and he was casual about keeping in touch with the office. But when he didn't turn up on Thursday we rang again, then we sent a man round in case he was ill. The flat was shut and he couldn't get in. So we rang to one or two likely places but again drew blank. We were getting a little worried by then and by noon on Friday we decided to act. We went to the police.'

'And what did they say?'

'That's the part of it none of us liked at all. After all

we're an official body and Campbell's a very important man. But we picked up an uneasy impression that the police knew something but wouldn't tell us.'

Charles Russell would have agreed with this, or at least with the first of the two assumptions; he would have agreed that the police almost certainly knew something but experience suggested strongly that it wasn't that they wouldn't tell. On the contrary they couldn't tell because orders had come from the top to say nothing.

Charles Russell repaid the other's candour. 'And what would you like me to do?'

'You would help?'

'James Campbell wasn't exactly a friend but he was a man I very much respected.'

'You have connections with the police, I think.'

'Guilty,' Charles Russell said at once. 'But when you say police what police did you go to?'

'We went to the top or as near as we could.'

'The name, if I may.'

The other man gave it.

'I know him and have sometimes worked with him. He won't refuse to see me, that's certain, but if what I suspect is true he may stall; he may tell me no more than he told to you.' Russell hesitated but finally said it. 'I don't like the smell of this a bit.'

'You're very kind.'

'I'm seldom that. Can I reach you at the Commission?'

'Surely.'

'Then I'll try and make an appointment this afternoon.'

Charles Russell made his appointment easily but

there the easy path ended in stone. His host received him in formal uniform, something he'd never done before. He had hung up his belt on a peg—the only concession. On the hatrack was his uniform cap, admirably kept, Russell noted. Russell had never seen him wear it.

The Assistant Commissioner asked politely: 'What can I do for Colonel Russell?'

The 'Colonel', Russell decided, was neutral. Both of them were a little too old for the incontinent use of Christian names. But the impersonal 'Colonel Russell' was ominous.

'James Campbell belonged to my club,' Russell said. He could have added 'And was my friend', but didn't. He had an accurate and punctilious mind.

'And you've heard that he hasn't been seen for three days? May I ask from whom?'

'Do I need to tell you?'

'No, I don't think you do—I can make a guess.'

'His interest is forgivable.'

'It depends on who is forgiving what.'

'Stop playing the fool,' Charles Russell snapped. It was a dangerous gambit to risk but it worked. For a moment this senior policeman looked abashed.

'I hate to treat you this way.'

'Then treat me sensibly.'

'You could ask me questions and perhaps I might answer. I'd answer Yes, No, or maybe No Comment.'

'Better than nothing,' Russell conceded. 'Then do you know where Campbell is?'

'To that one I answer No, we do not.'

'Do you suspect unusual circumstances?'

'No comment on that, I'm afraid.'

'Very well—understandable. Was anything found of significance?'

'No.'

'No fingerprints of known hoodlums?'

'No.'

'Were Campbell's clothes in order?'

'Yes.'

'Bed slept in?'

'Yes.'

'Had he packed a bag?'

'No comment again. I'm very sorry.'

Charles Russell rose and took his leave. He was annoyed but also sympathetic. This normally helpful senior policeman was acting under binding orders. They could only have come from a single source and that was a very frightened Minister. It might be the Home Secretary or it might be the old humbug himself. Whichever it was the motive was clear. They didn't want political trouble, they were terrified of another scandal. Rather than that they would write off Campbell.

Russell went to a phone booth and rang his acquaintance. He'd achieved exactly nothing whatever. He was more than sorry but there it was.

As he walked home he considered it carefully. He was certain James Campbell was no defector. Russell hadn't a valid reason for this, there'd been some odd and quite unexpected defections, but he was also prepared to trust his instinct. So Campbell was no traitor. . . . Therefore . . . Therefore James Campbell must have been snatched and therefore again . . .

Russell stopped thinking: someone was tailing him. It had happened before, he was pretty well used to it, but he liked it to be done professionally and the man behind him was well short of that. He was making no attempt at concealment but keeping a steady ten yards behind. When Russell went faster this man went faster and when Russell slowed he slowed down too. Russell stopped and turned and the man came up boldly. Charles Russell said: 'Can I help you, sir?'

'That's more than I'd hoped you would say.'

'But I do.'

The stranger wore the impersonal clothes which Russell by now could quickly recognize. He might be an embassy's chauffeur, its chef, but he could give the diplomats orders and see them obeyed. 'Could we go to your flat?' he inquired.

'By all means.'

The man moved a hand and a taxi drew up to them. It had been following twenty yards behind and Russell had spotted that too. They got in. Russell gave the address though this stranger would know it.

. . . I'm taking a bit of a risk, I suppose. It's conceivable somebody's snatching me too.

But he could see they were taking the proper route and the taxi drew up at his flat as instructed. The driver climbed down and opened the door for them.

. . . Very few genuine cabbies do that still.

They went upstairs: Russell opened the door. They fussed in the continental manner as to who should precede through the open door, but finally the stranger went first. Russell waved at a chair but the other stayed standing. 'Smith,' he said formally. 'Jacob Smith.' His English was almost but not quite perfect but Smith was quite certainly not his name. Nor, Russell was very sure by now, was tailing his normal occupation. He carried much heavier guns than that.

'Very well, Mr Smith—I must call you something.' Russell waved at a chair again. Both sat down.

'May I go back in time a little?'

'If it helps in whatever you wish to tell me.'

'Then I think you have been approached already by somebody much senior to me.'

'I was asked to take an active interest in a matter which I thought exaggerated.'

'Exaggerated? I'm afraid we're convinced you're very wrong. And you stuck to your decision firmly even when given a reason to change it.'

'If you mean about Belami Clark and Molina——'

'Escaping to a place called Neuwald. That didn't change your decision?'

'No.'

'Then perhaps this will.' Mr Smith leant forward. 'You probably know from your own good sources that a man called James Campbell has disappeared. You will also know what he does and is.' Mr Smith drew a deliberate breath. 'We believe that Campbell is now in Neuwald, in Molina's house and held there prisoner.'

Charles Russell was surprised, for once showed it. 'How do you know?'

'We do not know. I said "believe" and repeat "believe". But since I'm talking to a man in the business, one with an international standing'—he made a formal and exact little bow—'since I'm talking to Colonel Russell himself there's no damage in revealing the facts. Which are that we're interested in a certain old airfield and I'm fairly sure you know which one. And on Tuesday evening we were running a man out, a normal and routine operation. Except that an aircraft took off before ours did, and that was very abnormal indeed. More abnormal was an abandoned ambulance. One of our men took the number and checked it. It had been stolen from a depot in London the night James Campbell disappeared.'

'You're thorough,' Russell said admiringly.

'We thought it might have had a connection with some counter-operation against us so we satisfied ourselves that it hadn't.'

'Interesting.'

'And more to come. We have stringers, as you no doubt know, in most places which we consider sensitive, and the deplorably bourgeois country of Switzerland is for various reasons one of those. And on Wednesday evening there was a curious incident. A big black car was stopped on the frontier having gone through the French side without any trouble. The Swiss, being Swiss, are rather more thorough, but they let this car through without inspection. It was driven by a Japanese male nurse—passport quite in order, clean. There was also a British doctor—the same. They said there was a third man inside, a very rich Swiss going home to die. They showed a Swiss passport but nobody checked him. The blinds of the car were down, the man dying.'

'Very good planning,' Charles Russell said. 'But didn't they ask where this man meant to die?'

'Of course they did. The answer was Neuwald.'

'Which your very efficient stringer verified?'

'He telephoned to Mrs Monteath who I think you've been told is already *en poste* there.'

'I have indeed. And what did she do?'

'She checked up and found it unexpectedly easy. Molina's villa is screened by a wall and there are one or more South American bodyguards. But a road runs past it with trees alongside and Mrs Monteath could manage one of them. From that tree you can see the stable yard.'

'And in it she spotted a big black car?'

'She did just that. The number hadn't been taken—a slip—but they'd made one rather careless mistake. The blinds of that car were still drawn down.' Mr Smith smiled blandly and blew his nose. 'So I've been sent to repeat an invitation.'

But Charles Russell had already decided, if decided, he reflected regretfully, was a proper word for an action in anger. Or could it be simply conditioned reflex, the old hunter in his comfortable paddock, the sound of the horn beyond the woods? That wasn't a reassuring thought but it was futile to pretend to oneself that a lifetime could be set aside easily. Charles Russell asked simply: 'Have you made the arrangements?'

'There's a night flight at three.' Smith produced the ticket. 'A car will call for you here and another at Zurich, and Mrs Monteath will await you in Neuwald.'

'That's the best news I've had in a bad affair. Shall I see you at the airport?'

'Wiser not.'

But in fact they did meet again in the small hours. Smith touched Russell's arm as he went through to Departure. 'Fresh news,' he said, 'and I think you should have it. We were talking in terms of a strong suspicion that Campbell was being hidden in Neuwald. Now we have more than suspicion. We know.'

'How do you know?'

'La Monteath has seen him. And we think you should take a hard look at Lenterheims. In Neuwald you can hardly miss it since it employs a full four men out of five.'

Helen had indeed met Molina and she had done so in an unusual way. Molina himself had picked her up. She'd been sitting in the bar of the Bleiner waiting for something to happen and bored. A man had come in and sat down at a table. He ordered wine in good English but certainly wasn't.

What he saw was a woman of thirty-four, though in fact he was giving her two years' grace. She wasn't thin but nor was she stout, precisely the age group and type he liked best. An experienced eye had absorbed the details. It had noticed the clothes which were good but casual, a notable head of fair hair carefully kept, the fresh colouring which went well with the hair. She was wearing a wedding ring but no others. When she spoke to the barman Molina listened. There was the pale ghost of an American accent overlaid by what he thought might be Scots.

These cool observations were both of them right. What was left of her American speech was the accent of the New England seaboard and the suspicion of her Scottish burr had come from her unregretted husband. He'd been a northern laird with a broken-down castle and he'd died of an injudicious mixture of his native whisky and sassenach pills. He had also been very much older than Helen.

That was something which since his death she had remedied. Molina had thought her a fine healthy woman and Molina had again been right.

There'd been a mirror behind the bar and she'd looked in it. The man at the table was not a big one but he was well built and wiry and she'd noticed that he moved lightly and gracefully. His black hair was his own and so were his teeth. He was drinking a local wine with distaste but he hadn't the air that he couldn't buy better. The air he exuded was very different; he threw out an inescapable maleness and Helen was both bored and a woman.

She felt in her bag for a cigarette, then rummaged in it again for a match.

. . . The oldest gag in the book.

But it worked. The man came up to the bar with a match. He had looked the gold lighter type but he wasn't, which put him one up though he didn't know it. She could see him better now—a Latin. Latins were lousy lovers—or were they? Regretfully she'd have had to admit that that was a theory she'd never tested. He smelt slightly of an expensive soap. Not scent—she would have sent him packing. His short-sleeved shirt exposed his forearms, surprisingly strong for a man of his height. His hands were very clean and broad and strong.

He sat down on the stool beside her easily. She had liked it that he hadn't asked her. This man knew his business, he wasn't a bumbler.

'May I offer a drink?'

'That's very kind.'

. . . If he orders champagne he's going to spoil it.

But he didn't; he looked at her glass instead. 'Whisky and water, I think?'

'Correct.'

'I'll stick to the wine myself, if I may. It's a horrible brew but my doctor advises it.'

'He's knocked you off the hard stuff? But why? You look a very fit man to me.'

He smiled at her. 'That's rather charming. But it isn't that whisky does me much harm, it's simply that I find it puts weight on me.'

It was an excuse to look him up and down, to undress a man without giving offence. She said when this operation was over: 'I don't think you've got a pound to worry about.'

'Just as well,' he said, 'since women don't like it.'

It was an opening but she wasn't yet ready. 'Don't tell me you've come here to take the waters.' There was a spa ten miles away. It was infamous.

'No, I've never drunk those disgusting waters, but there are other reasons to come here—good ones. For one thing my excellent doctor lives here and for another I'm slightly mad on waterskiing.'

'You stay in this hotel, then?'

'Oh no. I've a villa here. You must see it one day.'

Again it was an opening and once again the lady declined it. Helen said nothing; Molina smiled. This wasn't a fish to take easy bait. He preferred them that way, it was much more interesting. It was also, in the end, a lot simpler.

'Would you care to dance?' he asked.

She got up.

In what they chose to call the palm lounge was what they chose to call an orchestra. There was a piano and a man with a fiddle, another with an arthritic saxophone and a woman with drums and no sense of rhythm. They made a thin uninspiring bleat and the acoustics of the glass roof were terrible. One or two couples were dancing already, German-Swiss and very correct indeed. The palms were dusty, the floor unsprung. Helen Monteath saw Molina recoil. 'I've never been in here before. If I'd known I wouldn't have asked you.'

'Let's try it.'

He took her in his arms and they danced. He danced very well in the Latin manner, light and precise on his feet but masterful. Before she'd arrived she'd been shown a photograph but in any case she was modestly sure that this was the authentic Molina. . . . The Spanish accent, the villa, the doctor. . . . Only the waterskiing surprised her. It seemed a very odd sport for an ex-dictator.

When the awful band stopped at last he released her. 'Would you care to risk a tango?'

'Show me.'

He put her in a cane chair politely and walked over to the rostrum lightly. He said something to the pianist who nodded. Helen noticed again that he hadn't flashed money; he had simply expressed a wish. Enough.

When the music started again they rose. They were alone on the floor now; he held her tighter. He didn't paw and he didn't take liberties but the message was perfectly clear. Helen welcomed it. When the tune was finished he said with a smile: 'An apology for the real thing, of course.'

'I realize that and thanks for the lesson.'

'With practice you would be very good anywhere.' His manner was more relaxed, he was confident. Helen Monteath did not resent it.

They went back to the bar and another drink and Molina looked at his watch. It was eight. 'Time for dinner,' he said, 'but not to eat here.'

Helen Monteath was in total agreement. The Bleiner was not her hotel, far from it. She'd been sent here under orders which she'd never considered disobeying, but she hadn't eaten a decent meal in several days of bitter boredom. The Bleiner tried to be international and international food was what you got.

'There's no proper restaurant here in Neuwald.'

'There's a French one ten miles up the lake—not bad—but I was going to suggest my house. Excuse me.'

He rose without awaiting an answer and told the porter to put through a call to his villa. He had a couple of matters to clear in advance, for if he had failed as his country's dictator it hadn't been for lack of foresight. The first of these matters was very simple, the order for the evening meal. He was bringing a guest, a woman of taste. Say an avocado pear with dressing, then a good *paella* with plenty of shellfish. Cheese on the side if needed afterwards.

It pleased him that his impression of Helen was of a woman who'd do good food a justice, and if she had to starve next day that wouldn't be hard at that terrible Bleiner.

But the second matter was rather more delicate. He was ringing to warn Clark—*get lost*. He hadn't believed that Clark would do it, not bring a snatched man to the villa and hide him there, for he'd decided after a day of reflection that Clark's so-called scheme had been an excuse to get money. But he'd seen the big black car arrive and Molina had had to think again.

So far Clark was within the limits laid down; he hadn't interfered with the household and he still had some days of the week permitted. After that Molina would throw them all out; he had more than paid his debt to Clark and in any case Clark had begun to annoy him. Clark had dismissed a Japanese but he'd imported an outlandish Dutchman. One couldn't take that for very long but nor did Molina intend to do so. Meanwhile he was bringing a woman to dinner and he didn't want anything looking irregular. . . . Understood? That was understood. So be it.

He returned to her and they drove to the villa. As Smith had already reported to Russell Helen Monteath had carefully recce'd it, and as they turned off a road in an opulent suburb her belief that this was Molina was certainty. Not that he hadn't surprised her greatly. She had expected something more florid and bumptious but he'd behaved with an almost English restraint. He even drove the fast little car with a prudence which was wholly admirable. He's no show-off, she thought—he doesn't need to be.

A servant, not Swiss, showed them into the villa. It was luxurious but again not vulgar.

'One more drink before dinner?'

'Perhaps just one.'

. . . He's not trying to make me tight—nothing hackneyed. I like that too, and after all why should he? He knows perfectly well that I'm going to say yes. I expect he prefers them sober. So do I.

They finished their drink and went to the dining-room. It was another surprise to Helen Monteath who'd expected portentous Spanish furniture. Instead it was excellent English Regency, dignified but airy and elegant. As they sat down at table Molina asked: 'Have you been here long?'

'About a week. Long enough to have picked up some local gossip.'

He understood her at once. 'So you've guessed who I am. I ought to have introduced myself.' He bowed across the table. 'Molina.'

66

'I'm Helen Monteath.'

'A very nice name. And you're not frightened of my political past?'

'Should I be frightened?'

'No, not at all. My failure, as I now understand, was a failure of a certain scrupulousness. If I'd had Spanish blood and nothing else I'd still be in my country today.' He looked at the servant who was serving the meal. 'That man is a pure South American Indian.'

'What of it?'

'He is also my cousin. A distant cousin but still a cousin.'

'It has made you a very handsome man.'

He gave her a smile and Helen hid one. Even the most intelligent men were susceptible to simple flattery.

He was relaxed but began to relax some more. 'You've been here a week? Alone? Aren't you bored?'

'I'm very bored indeed,' she said.

'Then why come to a place as dull as Neuwald? There are others more amusing and gayer.'

'The dullness is really the point.'

'I don't follow.'

'I've got something to forget, you see.' It was true as far as it went which wasn't far. Her last man had left her on edge and unsatisfied.

'The prescription wouldn't work with me but I think I can understand what you're saying. If you work yourself up to extremes of boredom then escape to your normal life is relief. But aren't you rather lonely?'

'Very.'

'I'm lonely too. You attract me greatly.'

. . . It's coming now. I wonder how. I'll hate it if he flounders about.

'One thousand pounds,' he said astonishingly.

Helen Monteath let her breath out contentedly. The orthodox reaction was settled: you drew yourself up to your full five feet eight and said something about not being a prostitute. Helen Monteath did neither of these. Duty, she thought, and its opposite pleasure. Traditionally they were supposed to be enemies and often, alas, that was what they were. Her duty was clear, she must know this man better, and bed was a solvent of most men's reserves. That she also felt sure she was going to enjoy it was a bonus which she hadn't expected. And she approved the direct approach, the straight buy. It saved such a mess of foolish words and a thousand was absurdly generous. Helen Monteath who should have been angry felt flattered and indeed rather lucky. To an agent it didn't break this way often but when it did the wise one rejoiced.

'In cash?' she said coolly.

He looked surprised. 'You'd prefer the usual gew-gaws?'

'No.'

'I didn't suppose you would.'

'That's rude.'

'On the contrary it's the highest compliment.' He rose and took her hand and kissed it. 'A woman who can take money gracefully is the nicest sort of woman of all.'

She woke in the night and stretched like a cat. He'd been a great deal more than merely experienced and she lay between the warm blankets happily. He'd left a light on in the adjoining bathroom and the door a few inches open. Expert. Helen looked round the luxurious room. She was certain this wasn't his normal bedroom—it was

68

as feminine as he was male—and she wondered, but without resentment, what woman had advised on its furnishing. The bed was enormous and very soft, and the underside of the canopy over it was looking-glass, an unbroken sheet of it. Two wall cupboards were full of nightdresses, of various sizes, three of each model. His seduction room, she thought, and a fine one. A little ornate to a protestant taste, but then this Latin would not be a protestant. He was a man with a sense of style, of fitness. He liked to do things well and he did.

He was sleeping beside her now, not snoring. His mouth was shut, he was breathing easily, sleeping as a baby slept, almost a conscious act of will. It would be a shame to disturb him by using the lavatory.

She'd noticed dressing-gowns in one of the cupboards but also that the house was well heated. She slipped out of bed in her dubious nightgown and walked down the corridor searching confidently.

Her confidence, she soon found, was misplaced: in fact she had simply lost her way. A door was half open and Helen pushed it. There was a night-light on and a man in a bed. There was also a man in a chair, half asleep. The eyes of the man on the bed were open, staring at the ceiling, unfocused. Helen who'd had to nurse her husband while he died of his mixture of pills and whisky could recognize the unmistakable, a man under very heavy sedation. The man's face she knew for she had seen it on telly.

She gasped and the man on the chair woke up. He was powerfully built and blond, very ugly, and he swore in a language strange to Helen. Then he moved behind her in three quick strides. He put his arms under hers and up again, locking his fingers behind her neck. He began to force her head down cruelly.

'Can you understand German?'

'Yes, a little.'

'Who are you then?'

'A friend of Señor Molina's.'

'That I can see,' he said contemptuously; he butted her in the nates rudely. 'You're a prostitute?'

'No.'

'I want more than that.'

He changed the full nelson to an old-fashioned armlock. She tried to turn against it. He held her and raised her elbow.

Helen Monteath screamed in bitter pain.

'I can dislocate your shoulder, you know. Tell me your business now or I will.'

He twisted again and again she screamed, then suddenly he let her go. He was lying on the floor in a heap and Molina was standing over him silently. Molina was wearing the lower half of a custom-made suit of black silk pyjamas and his naked flat chest had expanded in anger. He was carrying a brass-bound club and he spun this in his fingers reflectively.

'Very foolish to expose one's neck.' His voice was his conversational voice but it changed to concern as he asked her quietly: 'Did he hurt you much?'

'I don't think he's broken my arm but he hurt me.'

Molina looked down at the prostrate Dutchman, spinning the club in his fingers again. 'Would you like me to knock him about a bit?'

'I don't think that would do much good.'

'I quite agree—we are not barbarians.' He looked at the man on the bed and considered. James Campbell's eyes were open still but he hadn't turned his head to

70

watch them. Molina asked simply: 'You know that man?'

'I do,' she said. A lie would be a pointless evasion. He could always find out what he wished to know.

'And you came here to find him?'

'No, not precisely.' She hesitated but she knew who was winning. In any battle of wills with this strange little man she was going to come out of it second best. 'I'd been told he was here but I didn't go looking for him. I was looking for something rather different.'

'There's one—off the bedroom.'

'I know there is. But you were sleeping like a child and it's noisy.'

'That was really something more than considerate.' His voice was without a hint of sarcasm; he meant that she'd been very considerate; he waved a hand through the door at the outside corridor. 'The fifth on the left. I will wait for you here.'

When she came back he was standing silently. The Dutchman had moved but he wasn't yet conscious. 'So you're an agent,' Molina said. 'I'd suspected it.'

'Then why bring me here?'

'Why ever not?' This time his voice was simply astonished.

'It was a risk, you know.'

'I have taken much greater. On gambles which I considered good ones.' He looked at her with a bedfellow's smile. It was a very male smile but it wasn't impertinent. 'Tell me,' he said, 'have you ever acted?'

'On the stage, you mean?'

'I mean just that.'

'I've never been on the stage.'

'That is all I wanted to know. That is good. So this

incident is formally closed. Whatever you choose to tell your employer is a matter which in no way concerns me. I will tidy my own loose ends tomorrow. Meanwhile, I suggest we go back to our room.'

He gave her his arm and they walked down the corridor. Helen Monteath was a biggish woman and she knew that giggling didn't suit her. But at this moment she was gravely tempted. . . . She was for all practical purposes naked and a half-pyjama'd man she had slept with was leading her back to his bed unprotesting. She was an agent: he had waved it aside. She was holding his arm with a certain punctilio. They processed along the corridor with an air of almost official propriety. He could have been squiring her to some rather grand dinner, white tie and decorations, the lot.

She suppressed the giggle but not the thought. Only one prop to this scene was lacking, a string orchestra scraping away in the background.

It would be playing conversational Mozart.

5

Molina woke finally late next morning. Helen Monteath had already gone, but that didn't disturb him, she had said she rose early, and they'd made an appointment to meet for lunch. She had dressed very quickly and asked for a taxi, but a car had appeared at once instead. It carried her back to the Bleiner smoothly where her usual waiter served her breakfast and accepted the urgent message she left him. He was her radio link, a well trained operator, but his channel didn't open till noon. Naturally he transmitted in cypher, and this and the process the other end meant the General had been pressed for time. He had already told Smith to contact Russell again, but Helen's fresh news must be passed on too, confirmation that Campbell was really in Neuwald. So the General had signalled to London *Immediate* and at the airport Smith had just caught Charles Russell.

Molina who'd risen two hours behind Helen had said he had had loose ends to tidy and he proceeded to tie them up with decision. He received Clark in his severe-looking study and again he left him standing awkwardly. And he didn't mince his words; he spat them.

'Last night,' he said, 'was a clear breach of contract. I said you could go or stay as you pleased and you chose to stay on conditions agreed. One was that your prisoner must be out of my house within a week and the other that neither I nor my household should in any way be interfered with. Instead of which a guest of mine is assaulted by that preposterous guard of yours.'

'He exceeded his instructions grossly.'

'I don't care a damn what instructions you gave him. The understanding was breached and that is enough.'

'I'm sorry,' Clark said. He hated apologizing.

'Your regret neither moves me nor changes my mind. Since you've broken one term of the understanding I am fully entitled to alter the other. You will leave within three days. That is final. You and that barbarian guard of yours and the man upstairs who's the cause of this scandal.' Molina rose from behind his desk. 'Seventy-two hours and I mean it.'

'Very well,' Clark said mildly since he couldn't do otherwise. He hadn't the least intention of going but this wasn't the moment to show his hand. 'And what do I do in the next three days?'

'I should think you could use them to make your arrangements, but if you've spare time you must use it naturally. Whatever were your habits follow them.'

'May I go to the club?'

'What club?'

'The Aqua Club.'

'I didn't know you waterskied.'

'I don't but I've begun to learn.' Instinctively he had looked for cover. A man needed an ostensible reason to be in a town as dull as Neuwald.

For the first time Molina appeared to hesitate. 'I'm going there myself this morning.'

'You'd prefer that I didn't seem to know you?'

'I wouldn't prefer. I simply insist on it.'

'Very well,' Clark said again, unsmiling. Unsmiling

but he was hiding a smile. This degenerate little ex-dictator had no idea what was going to hit him.

When Clark had gone Molina relaxed. He took the fast car but again drove sedately, down to the town to visit his doctor. He hadn't troubled to make an appointment for he was a favoured patient both rich and appreciative. The receptionist asked him to wait five minutes, but she showed him not to the general waiting-room but to the doctor's very private study. As they walked past the door of the former it opened. A man came out on crutches, listlessly. It seemed that he couldn't use them properly. He looked pale and drained and wholly hopeless. Something had gone out of him. Life.

When Molina reached the doctor's surgery he shook hands with a continental formality, then almost grinned as he looked at Molina. He was French-speaking Swiss though he practised in Neuwald and he was roughly Molina's age, an old friend.

'For a man who's just had a political setback you're looking extremely fit and well.'

'You're looking the same yourself and I'm glad. But then you possess the secret of youth which you sell at an exorbitant price.'

The doctor wasn't offended; he laughed. 'Before we discuss the age-old dream take your clothes off and I'll check you over.'

He did so thoroughly, taking his time. 'Ticker as sound as a bell, pressure normal. Lungs clean as a whistle, no sugar in urine. I can't think why you waste my time.'

'You know very well why I waste your time.'

'Don't tell me you want another boost.'

'I want one and I've come to get it.'

'Jesus, you're a glutton for punishment.'

'It depends what you mean by punishment.'

'Women.'

'I beg to dissent and very firmly.'

'If you've found something sixteen and quite unsuitable I consider it rather less than dignified. I'm not even sure I'm prepared to treat you.'

'She's thirty-something, the prime of life. But I'm fifty-three—you know that well.'

'At fifty-three you do pretty nicely.'

'Not a reason not to continue doing so.'

The doctor sighed but went to a cabinet. Molina had put on most of his clothes. 'Roll up your sleeve.'

Molina did so.

As the doctor slid the needle in he said almost to himself: 'You're lucky.'

'And you are a very good friend and doctor.'

'Perhaps. But in certain matters helpless. Did you see a man outside on crutches? I cannot help him. Nobody can.'

'I think I can guess.'

'Yes, but quite wrongly.' The doctor was suddenly blazingly angry. 'Have you ever heard of Lenterheims?'

'Of course I have, it's here in Neuwald. It's some sort of chemical works.'

'And more.'

'I don't understand you.'

'And maybe as well. From my point of view the place is a menace. The precautions they take are quite exemplary and well beyond any legal requirements but men are all human and so sometimes careless. That man on the crutches was only careless but he's the third case

I've had this year. All will die.'

'I still don't understand you.'

'Good.' The doctor's anger had faded abruptly. He dabbed at the prick on Molina's arm. 'I gather you're staying up at your villa.'

'Yes, perhaps permanently. And I hope you will come to dinner.'

'With pleasure.'

Molina took his car again and this time drove to meet Helen Monteath. He had suggested the Aqua Club at noon, not because he intended to lunch there—the food was just as bad as the Bleiner's—but because there was a pleasant glassed terrace which looked out on the lake and the plage and the waterskiing. In the boring little town of Neuwald this was the only place with some style, for its patrons came mostly from outside Switzerland and the terrace was noisy with more than one language.

Helen arrived and chose gin and tonic. Molina was already on wine. He noticed that she had dressed with some care, nothing formal but also more than casually. This pleased him, it showed a sense of occasion, and women with a sense of that were less common than the glossies suggested. She looked out across the lake with interest.

'Quite an establishment.'

'Yes, I suppose so. In its way you could almost call it famous. Very good skiers come here to use it.'

'You're one of them, I imagine.'

'No. I'm competent now but I'm far from first class.' She was certain he was understating. In some ways he was almost English.

'Is it hard to learn?'

77

'It is at first.' He pointed to a man in the basin. He could see that it was Belami Clark and he was making very heavy weather. There was a launch with a boatman, obviously bored, and he was trying to get Clark up on his skis. As often as not he failed to do so, and when he did there was little worth watching. Clark would stagger and sway for perhaps ten yards, then fall with an untidy splash. He'd swim back to the basin, the launch would turn, and the performance would start again ignominiously.

Helen said on an impulse before she'd considered it: 'Show me how it's really done.'

'I wasn't thinking of skiing this morning.' In fact he'd intended to rest himself quietly. 'Putting it simply I'm not short of exercise.'

'I'm sorry if I've been tactless.'

'No.' He had changed his mind, he'd been challenged openly. Besides, he had been to his doctor. 'Come with me.'

He led her downstairs and unlocked a cabin, putting her in a chair while he changed. Helen looked round; she was quietly impressed. Molina was more than a casual customer. There'd been no talking and no obvious orders but a man had appeared with a choice of skis and a launch was already backing in.

When he came out he looked well in his wet-suit, muscular and lean and balanced. 'Just a short run,' he said, 'and nothing fancy.' He added with his agreeable irony: 'For the exercise which I do not need.'

He was up at once in the wake of the launch and she could see that he had indeed understated. She knew nothing of this curious sport but she knew what was good by simple instinct. He was out in the open water now, criss-crossing the tumbling wake, sometimes swinging away on the beam of the boat. He did this for perhaps ten minutes, then signalled for the launch to turn. When in shallow water he dropped the tow rope, coming in for the last few yards without it, sinking expertly up to his waist, still standing. The skis floated up and an attendant collected them. Molina waded ashore; he was smiling.

'I hope you enjoyed it.'

'I did indeed.'

'Because I don't know anyone else I'd have done it for.'

He changed again and they went back to the terrace. He looked at his watch. 'It's time for luncheon. I'll take you to that place up the lake.'

'I ate an enormous meal last night. If I eat another I'll get as fat as a pig.'

'I prefer you as you are,' he said. 'Very well, we'll have an omelette here.' The skiing had made him distinctly hungry but if she wanted to starve he would have to starve too.

They ate sparingly and went back to the car. As he drove he said casually: 'I have something to show you.'

'And I've got something to show to you.'

She produced from her handbag a fat sealed envelope. She had found it as she left that morning. Very smooth, she had thought, very tactful and expert. But the seal was still unbroken, intact.

'I can't take this.'

'You'd prefer a cheque?'

'You're teasing me. I'm not going to take it.'

He said stubbornly: 'I made a promise. I like to keep them.'

'You didn't promise you'd give me pleasure.'

'That's something no wise man likes to promise.'

She held out the money again. 'I won't take it. If *you* won't I'll throw it out of the car.'

He laughed at her. 'The purest melodrama. Keep it for half an hour and then see. Maybe you'll want a new set of curtains.'

'What on earth do you mean?'

'I mean what I say. I told you I had something to show you.'

In the town they stopped outside an office and Molina went in with an air of decision. 'I'll have to get the key,' he explained.

They drove on through the featureless suburbs, going uphill. At the top of the rise the buildings had thinned—little chalets now in formal gardens. Molina stopped outside one and handed her out. He opened the door with his key. They went in.

It was simply but rather beautifully furnished and the prints on the wall said the owners were English.

'I expect you would like to see the kitchen.'

Helen, in a daze, saw the kitchen.

'The heating is efficient too. In Switzerland it has to be. This chalet belongs to some people I know and it's for rent for as long as you care to use it.'

'You want me to move in here?'

'Very much. It's more comfortable than the Bleiner, isn't it?'

'You're setting me up *dans mes meubles?*'

'Just so.' He could have added but it would have sounded pompous that he had learnt by now how to treat a lady. Instead he waved an airy hand. 'Naturally I will make all arrangements.'

'But you know I'm an agent.'

'Why not finish your mission?'

'You're serious?'

'Of course I am.'

'But when would you want me to move?'

'At once.'

She looked out of the window. The garden was charming. She said with her back still turned: 'And tonight?'

'I will call for you and take you to dinner.'

Half an hour before he came and did so Helen's own instructions arrived. Colonel Russell had agreed to join her and she was to put herself under his orders unquestioningly. A car had been arranged at the airport but she wasn't to meet him there herself. He'd been booked at the Bleiner, a single room, and he'd casually pick her up next day as though they had never met before. Helen was pleased and even excited. She knew Charles Russell and also liked him. And he wouldn't arrive till tomorrow morning. Tactful of him, she thought. Considerate. Or more likely it was just a good break. When you started to get them they trod on your heels.

Charles Russell on his uncomfortable aircraft had been unable to sleep, which was most unusual, but he had a logical mind and uncertainty troubled it. Clark's plan, or the Colonel-General's reading of it, had a savage and faintly dotty simplicity but it mustn't be despised for that. Simplicity at any level was the mark of the experienced planner, and for two great Powers to destroy each other, one of them the Power Clark hated, was something which could happen anyway if some idiot made a miscalculation. That was Clark's premise and all too tenable. So in effect what Belami Clark intended was simply to throw a match in the powder keg. The match would be overwhelming suspicion that the Germans were making a nuclear weapon. That would take some building up, much money, but if the Russians took the bait they would act. Charles Russell hadn't a doubt of that.

As a matter of very simple reasoning the position was so far alarmingly clear, but the uncertainty was the other great Power. For if she turned her back there would be no war, no war and therefore no subsequent tragedy. Charles Russell frowned: it was anyone's guess. The great Power in question had lost much face, no client believed in her bond or word, but two factors might force her reluctant hand. In which case Clark would see his holocaust.

The first factor was Russian military dogma to which limited war was the great anathema. Russell, a soldier, understood perfectly. If you had to go in then you went in totally. No dropping of paratroops, then a quick withdrawal, but your power to enforce your will used finally. They'd been very frank and indeed why not? On their flanks they'd use chemical warfare to cover them, and in the centre, where they'd chosen their corridor, they'd come through with massed armour regardless of losses.

Then how would the other great Power react? Charles Russell shrugged for he didn't know. It had tactical atomic weapons but if it used them he knew very well what would happen. New York would not go up in smoke, but Birmingham would or Bordeaux or Düsseldorf. And would America risk her own cities for these? Charles Russell, like General de Gaulle, thought she wouldn't. But she'd have troops on the ground, now disordered, retreating, so what risk would be taken to save a debacle? Ten divisions in the bag—intolerable. America might be withdrawing her frontiers, she was tiring of an ungrateful Europe, but she was still a proud and powerful nation. Even the most supine of Presidents could have his hand forced by furious public opinion. So only a choice had now emerged: Belami Clark might have got it wrong, in which case he would be disappointed, but he couldn't be proved to have got it wrong, and if he happened to have got it right then Belami Clark was the West's first enemy. That wasn't an exaggeration.

Charles Russell fell into sleep at last, but he wouldn't if he could have seen to the east of him. For the General was up against the wall, the sense of the meeting strongly against him. The political member was asking dangerously: 'So they've snatched this man Campbell and are holding him in Neuwald?'

The Colonel-General had nodded briefly.

'Campbell who's just returned from America, where we know there have been alarming developments?'

'I don't think that these recent developments cover making a Bomb in some backyard garage.'

'No?' The political member was less than friendly.

The military member came in on his side. 'Backyard garage—very probably not. But you will know what exists at Neuwald. Lenterheims.'

'Agreed,' the Colonel-General said.

'That agreement should be noted for record.' All these men were very expert in-fighters. They had to be or they sank without trace.

'Then what do you propose?'

'More inquiries.'

'To what end?'

'The true facts.'

The chairman intervened at once. 'Reasonable, but not open ended.' He turned to the Colonel-General directly. 'We will give you ten days from this moment precisely. After that we shall have to plan for action.'

And at the other end of a shrinking world the same two men sat in the oval room, the same two men and again in hostility. The chunky man was saying angrily: 'You've simply got to listen, and carefully.'

'I don't want to know.'

'You mistrust my sources?'

'No, it isn't that, they're as good as anybody's.'

'Believe me, there's something dangerous brewing.'

'And a Convention here just round the corner.'

Chunky who was head of an Agency, who had no fences to mend across a continent, no machine which might not re-adopt him, shook a finger at the other man's desk.

'Someone once said "The Buck Stops Here".'

'I'm not from Missouri. I don't make folksy cracks but I keep my cool. Nothing's yet happened—come back when it does. It's a mistake to think that because you can't panic me I'll chicken if we're slapped in the face.'

The chunky man rose and packed his briefcase. He had a passion for planning, mistrusted pragmatics. 'God help us all,' he had said as he left.

Charles Russell woke just before the dawn. He was stiff and unrested but also expectant. He looked forward to seeing Helen again, a woman whom he'd once nearly employed. She'd been told to accept his orders unquestioningly, but he seldom banged out orders brutally; he preferred to work in harness and smoothly. In any case he didn't yet know what orders would be at this moment appropriate. There was the matter of Campbell, that surely came first, and afterwards there was the other of Lenterheims. He'd been asked to take a very hard look at it, and a man like Smith wouldn't say that for nothing. Nor had he given a hint; that was sensible. If Lenterheims was of any importance Smith and his master the Colonel-General would wish it viewed with unprejudiced eyes. Unprejudiced but also experienced. For that was why Russell was on this aircraft. Experience and a certain detachment.

Lenterheims, Charles Russell thought. The name rang a bell but he couldn't tag it.

6

Russell's flight had been delayed as usual and he didn't
find Helen Monteath till midday. They exchanged their
information quickly. He had met her before and
thought well of her then, indeed at one moment he'd
considered employing her. But in the event he had
turned her down on principle. The good agent, like the
good civil servant, was as near a-political as his nature
would let him be. He certainly wasn't actively Right as
Helen Monteath had now become.

A curious story, Russell remembered, very different
from the conventional pattern. As head of the Security
Executive he'd been familiar with this too often to
please him, the rich woman with an uneasy conscience
trying to salve it by drifting away to the Left and the
shadowy world of imagined Causes. But Helen had
never been rich—not at all. When her husband had died
there'd been almost no money, and his estate, for the
little it still was worth, had only been his for his single
lifetime. She would have wished to work however
comfortable and she'd come south to London to try to
find it.

She had found it in the world of broadcasting, and at
once its peculiar aura had tainted her, the producers
convinced of their social message which they inflicted
on their captive audiences with the merciless zeal of a
Grand Inquisitor, the rich actors financing some way-

out Party. There was an unspoken slant against all things established, the army, the church, the crown, the police. If you queried it you were stared at incredulously and if you openly rowed against the stream you didn't get any form of promotion. You could even quietly lose your job.

Helen Monteath had not done that. She needed the money, she went along, and in time she'd become like many others, the bright skin of what Russell called Fancy Left and a core inside which she didn't dare look at. Till one night of an almost Damascene conversion. She'd been watching an unsuccessful play. It was a message play or she wouldn't have been at it, for she'd been taught to despise all commercial theatre. The star who was also a competent actress had been ranting about some pig of a policeman who'd been caught in an act of admitted corruption. Not that that had been the serious crime. His real offence was not the corruption—it went without saying all police were corrupt—but the fact that the high-thinking victim had been a journalist on a left-wing paper. Moreover the unfortunate man had been coloured. The Inspector had therefore been under orders, sinister orders from a sinister source. No proof had been asked for and far less adduced. The Enemies of the People were everywhere.

Helen had left the theatre quietly, then gone to a pub and had drunk too much. Next day she had found another job a very long way from the world of the media, and for something like three months she'd read seriously. This had fortified the sudden conversion: one needn't be unresistingly brainwashed by a foolish clique mouthing shallow ideas. There was a case for another view and a good one. Then one day at a party she'd met

Charles Russell. She knew what he did though she wasn't supposed to and the new job she had found had begun to bore her. She had asked if she might come and see him.

He had received her warily but also with interest. In television she'd only been one of many who hadn't rated a file in his office, but he'd made some inquiries and knew her past background. He'd been curious what she could want of Charles Russell.

He soon found out: she wanted to work for him. He had turned her down politely at once but the refusal had nagged him for several days. He couldn't employ her, he dare not employ her, but he was experienced in assessing people and as an agent Helen Monteath had potential. She was old enough to have grown out of foolishness, not old enough to have lost her gusto; she was an intelligent and a handsome woman. And now she was in open revulsion from what Russell himself despised as she did. She was too good to waste, she was high-class material. So if she'd swung from the soft, soft Left with some violence why not put her in touch with the hard, hard Right? Which in Russell's opinion was orthodox communism. It was hated and feared by the new elite but he'd begun to believe in its ultimate victory. For it had what the new thinkers lacked; it had discipline. It had an empire and a real foreign policy; it thought, as men should, from accepted premises, unblinded by a cloudy humanism. Helen Monteath it might train and fulfil.

He'd considered it for some time very carefully, then passed Helen's name to his friend the General. He knew it was an unorthodox action but it seemed to him to be perfectly logical.

Logical and therefore right. All other values were at bottom subjective.

And today she had orders to take his own, though that was not how he intended to treat her. He listened to her recital carefully. It was succinct and entirely impersonal.

. . . They've trained her very well indeed.

'So you've contacted Molina?'

She nodded.

'And Molina suspects you're an agent?'

'He said so.'

'But he didn't throw you out?'

'Far from it.'

'He sounds a rather remarkable man as you are a remarkable woman. But has he mentioned your seeing Campbell that night?'

'He told me the matter was closed. He has kept to it.'

'Then we'll consider that aspect later if necessary. For the moment the urgent problem is Campbell—how to release him and where to put him.'

'You don't think they're torturing him?'

'No, I would doubt it.' Charles Russell considered, then gave his reason. 'If your master the Colonel-General is right, they're not after knowledge, which wouldn't serve them, but our *suspicion* of a knowledge which would. Which reminds me—we should keep to our brief. If the Colonel-General is right again all this is a gigantic poker game. However convincing they make the scenery we mustn't be bluffed into tamely accepting it. If something occurs which we're *sure* is not bluff it's our business to report the fact, after which I'd prefer not to think of the consequences, but if that doesn't happen we've had our instructions. Which in short are to expose a set-up, to convince naturally anxious men that it is one.'

She nodded again. 'I agree. But Campbell?'

'Campbell is our first objective. Have you any ideas?'

'Not very good ones. The obvious course is to go to the police, or with you here to somebody more important. They'd pull out Campbell all right but that would blow everything. The Swiss have a weakness for all rich men but a horror of international involvement. So they'd give us back Campbell but throw us all out—Molina and his household and you and me. And then we'd be back where we started, nowhere. Just some other place and some other time . . .'

'Clear thinking,' Russell said. 'And your plan?'

'I'm afraid I don't have one.'

'May I ask questions?'

'Certainly. I'm here to answer them.'

'Then you say that Molina knows you're an agent but that that hasn't ended your pleasant relationship. The deduction from that, if indeed there is one, is that he's not actively backing whatever Clark's up to.'

'That's my own impression for what it's worth, but I suspect Clark has some sort of hold on Molina.'

'Then we'll go to the villa and *ask* for Campbell. If what you say and I think are right then Molina may very well hand him over, and if he doesn't or is prevented from doing so we shall know where we stand, which is deep in trouble. For the conclusion we'd have to draw from that is that they really want Campbell for something technical, not simply as part of a plan to deceive us. In which case we'd have to report accordingly, in which case I'm very sorry for Europe.'

'Let's hope you're right.'

'If I prayed I would do so. But there's still the question of where to put him. I gave a reason for thinking they won't be torturing him but from what you tell me he's heavily drugged. We can't put him into a local nursing home without raising every sort of question.'

'I can solve that one,' she said.

'You can?'

'I'm not living in this hotel any more. We can put him in my house.'

'You have one?'

'Molina has set me up in style.'

He looked at her with a real admiration. 'You're a very good soldier,' he said at last.

'A compliment but not a deserved one. I'm really getting quite fond of Molina.' She looked at her watch: it was close on lunch-time. 'Should we go now?'

'No, certainly not. We're not something out of television, we're not going armed and our weapon is reason. And the deeper into the day you get the weaker the average man reacts to it. But catch him early enough after breaking his fast and even the stupid are sometimes rational.' Russell spoke with conviction, he had learnt by experience. 'So we'll go tomorrow morning at ten. But there's something for this afternoon. Did your friends mention anything here called Lenterheims?'

'They did but I wasn't to case the joint.' She smiled. 'I was to leave that to you.'

'We can't do that now without making a plan but I wouldn't mind having a general look-see.'

'You can see it from the hill past my chalet.'

'Where no doubt you will offer a cup of tea.'

They drove up the hill in the small fast car which she'd found earlier in the chalet's garage. Charles Russell didn't remark on it. He'd paid her his compliment once. Enough. So they drove up the hill and stopped at the top of it. The complex of Lenterheims lay below them and Russell quartered it through powerful fieldglasses. 'There's a section behind a double fence. I can see men patrolling the outer one regularly and there are watchtowers at each corner with searchlights. I can't be sure but I think I see guard dogs.'

'Heavy security,' Helen said.

'James Campbell, if we get him out, should be able to throw some light on that.'

They drove back to the Bleiner after tea in the chalet. Russell was too worldly wise to have wasted breath suggesting they dine together, so he let her return to Molina's chalet and later to a pleasant evening. He hadn't a doubt of that: she looked happy. Women agents met disagreeable duties but Helen Monteath hadn't worn the air of a woman grimly doing her duty.

He let her go and bathed again, thinking as the warm water relaxed him that as days went this had been rather a good one. But at the back of his mind was that troubling bell still. It was ringing but the sound sent no message.

Lenterheims—he'd been told to look at it. Lenterheims—he had heard that before.

The Dutchman was boring Clark severely but he was obliged to listen—the man sometimes had something. 'That woman,' he was saying now, 'the one who burst into Campbell's room.'

'You mean when Molina clubbed you?'

The Dutchman flushed. The incident had hurt his pride and he hadn't an excuse which held water. 'I had my back to him,' he said.

'So you told me before but never mind that. What's new about this woman, then?'

'I'm sure she's an agent.'

'That too you have told me. But why are you sure?' Privately Clark longed to be sure. Snatching an eminent nuclear scientist had been designed to startle Security's dovecotes and sooner or later he was bound to be traced. If this woman was in fact an agent then the plant had begun to bear fruit very promptly.

'I've been making inquiries down in the town. Molina picked her up at the Bleiner.'

'Molina picks up many women.'

The Dutchman ground on with a massive stolidity; he was as difficult to stop as a tank. 'She was staying at the Bleiner alone and she isn't a bad-looking woman. Moreover she doesn't waterski.' The Dutchman lowered his heavy head. 'Now why should a woman, good looking, alone, a woman with no interest in waterskiing—why should such a one go to the Bleiner at all?'

'You have a point.'

'I know I have.' It sounded smug but the Dutchman was.

'But it isn't proof the woman's an agent.'

'Then why is she there with another agent?' The Dutchman grinned, he had played his trump, and playing it had given him pleasure. Clark's leadership he'd accepted freely but he didn't always care for his manner. He thought it offhand and at times plain

93

arrogant. His plan was a good one but he wasn't a comrade.

Clark who'd been bored was suddenly interested. 'What other agent?'

'A man called Charles Russell.'

'Who was head of the Security Executive?'

'That's the one.'

'You're sure of that?'

'Of course I am—I saw them leave together. Incidentally in one of Molina's cars.'

'I meant are you sure the man is Russell.'

'I recognized him,' the Dutchman said crossly. He'd expected warm congratulations, not to be cross-examined closely.

'That implies you have met him.'

'Yes, I have. They picked me up once on a job in London and that Russell grilled me—much worse than you are. Naturally I gave nothing away but two days later I woke up outside England. I dare say they could have done much worse but you know what odd laws the English have.'

'Thank you, you may go,' Clark said.

When the Dutchman had done so Clark broke a rule; he poured a celebratory drink since this news deserved a high celebration. It was working, it was really working. The *mise-en-scène* was building up. He had intended that the world Security services should be biting their nails and demanding instructions and now at least one country had given them. An agent here already? Excellent. But the ex-head of the Security Executive was something a great deal more than an agent. Clark hadn't dared hope for results so soon. They were worried, were they? Better than excellent. And they'd be something more than biting their nails when James Campbell's body was found in the lake.

For what was the natural conclusion from that? That he'd betrayed what he knew under wicked duress and thus wasn't of any further use to the men who now possessed his knowledge. And men who had secrets must mean to use them.

They wouldn't like that, they wouldn't indeed. Any subsequent developments would begin to look much more than suspicious and Clark had planned these developments thoroughly. He'd had all of thirty years to do so, to plan to bring down the pillars finally.

So the promptness of this Russell's arrival was a stroke of good fortune he hadn't expected. Clark knew something of drugs but he wasn't a doctor and he couldn't keep Campbell sedated for ever. If he misjudged a matter he wasn't expert in Campbell could die in his bed in this villa. Which would not only compromise Clark's base (he thought of it as *his* base—damn Molina) but miss the impact of what he'd always intended, the body of a top nuclear scientist found floating in a cold Swiss lake.

That would have them all running in febrile circles, anxious and ready to credit the worst. Caution would decrease with suspicion, good judgement decay in the face of credulity. That was only a part of the plan, a starter, but it wouldn't get out of the gate without Campbell.

Clark decided to go upstairs and look at him. He was injected in the early morning, which gave the Dutchman eleven hours off duty, and four hours ago they had given the dose. In the evening he woke and they fed and washed him, then another but lighter dose for the night.

James Campbell was lying, as always, motionless, but this time his eyes were closed in sleep. Clark nodded and left him. All seemed normal.

But it wasn't quite normal for Campbell was foxing. His eyes weren't closed in innocent sleep but to hide any hint of renascent intelligence. Like Belami Clark he wasn't a doctor but he was a scientist with some knowledge of chemistry and he could make good if by no means certain guesses both as to what they'd used to snatch him and also as to what they used now. The latter wasn't a knock-out but clearly a sedative, a powerful one and therefore tricky. They couldn't continue with massive doses unless they intended to kill him in bed, and in moments of lucidity Campbell could see no good motive for doing so.

And these moments of lucidity were increasing in number and also in strength. For Campbell was over-reacting deliberately. He had guessed they would have to lower the doses: they'd lower them more if he acted a little. His tolerance to the drug was increasing: all he need do was pretend that it wasn't. The early-morning injections still put him out but by ten o'clock he was something like conscious, conscious enough at any rate to have put on a little act that morning when Belami Clark had come up to look at him. And some afternoons he was almost normal, weak as a kitten but close to human. One afternoon he had even got up, staggering to the window and looking out. The drop was maybe forty feet, reduced if he could hang on the window sill, and there was a flower bed below with thickish shrubs. He might break a leg or again he might not. That wasn't, as he saw it, the difficulty: the difficulty was the matter of timing. It was pointless to jump out of a window for the Dutchman to pick him up ignominiously. He'd only earn himself much bigger injections. He'd have to choose a propitious moment when somebody else's car was outside and chance that whoever was in that car was the sort of man he hoped he would be.

Not much of a plan, James Campbell decided, but it was better than lying here indefinitely. They hadn't tortured him or even asked questions. He was grateful for that.

It was also ominous.

Belami Clark couldn't read these thoughts or he would certainly have returned with the needle. At this moment he was sending messages. In Ulm he had contacted eight men. One of them he had had to kill; the Japanese who had helped him to kidnap Campbell he'd sent back to his normal base in Germany; and the Dutchman was already with him. So there were still six men whom he had to call up for the final and decisive move. Six men whom a decadent world called criminals. It wasn't too many and it might be too few.

Too few and by no means ideal choices. The corners of Clark's mouth turned down wryly. All these men had murdered, sabotaged, stolen, but he had little respect or none at all for the philosophy and mystique of mere terrorism. These men would obey since Clark held the purse strings and without money or arms they could do very little, but except for the elder Japanese he hadn't dared tell them the whole of his plan.

He relaxed as he thought of it—yes, it was good. He'd had thirty years to hone and polish it, and the last wrench on the nerves of the men he was racking would be something in which he felt justified pride. But he hadn't been able to share his pleasure with the other five men whom he now commanded. If that, he thought, was a proper word. They were desperate and no doubt committed, they would never dilate or draw back in fear, but they lacked even an elementary discipline, and if Belami Clark were to try to impose it he knew what would happen at once. They would leave him.

Poor instruments for a plan so excellent. Nevertheless they were all he had.

He sent six messages to six different drops. All of them said the same. They said: *Gather*.

Helen called at the Bleiner next morning for Russell at a quarter to ten for ten at the villa. She'd enjoyed her first night at the neat little chalet and Molina had approved of his breakfast. She had told him she didn't need a cook. She had to have something to do in the daytime.

'I thought you worked as an agent,' he'd said.

'I shan't for very much longer, I hope.'

'That is excellent news.' He had waved it aside again.

So Helen collected Russell punctually and they climbed into the little red car. 'You're looking very well,' Russell said.

'I'm feeling very well indeed.'

'Any news from your gentleman friend about Campbell? I can forgive you for forgetting it but the object of this excursion of ours is to remove him from Molina's house. It would help if we knew Molina's attitude to the fact that James Campbell is there at all.'

'He simply declines to discuss the matter. I've asked him outright who that man in the bed was and all he will say is: "What man? That is finished."'

'As I said once before Molina's remarkable.'

'He's a very unusual man indeed. I suspect that I'm getting more than to like him.'

Charles Russell let this pass without comment. 'And did you mention the matter of using the chalet to hide James Campbell if we're successful in springing him?'

'Yes, I did, though I didn't use Campbell's name.'

'And what did he say?'

'He said what I expected he'd say. He said that the chalet was mine, not his, and if I chose to invite a guest I was free to. If the guest was male that was somewhat irregular, but if the man was who he thought he might be his health was probably less than robust and in the circumstances he wouldn't be jealous. In any others he'd feel obliged to kill him.'

'Quite a man.'

'Oh, he's that. And as I told you before he knows I'm an agent but I've hinted I'm on a limited mission. Limited in time, that is. Anything that helps to end it will be very much O.K. with Molina.'

'And how are you going to introduce me?'

'That doesn't arise—he won't be there. He'll be waterskiing down at the Aqua Club.'

Charles Russell frowned. 'That's disappointing. Our weapon, as I told you, is reason, and the more I hear of your friend Molina the more reasonable he seems to be. But as it breaks we'll be facing Clark and that Dutchman. The latter sounds pretty thick in the head and the former is a committed man. I know that total commitment is fashionable but it's seldom, in my experience, reasonable.'

'There's an alternative,' Helen Monteath said thoughtfully.

Russell looked at her handbag. 'I forbid it formally.

That's the only order I mean to give you but I've given it and it *is* an order.'

'How did you know I had a gun?'

'I can smell them a mile away by now.'

'I can use it, you know.'

'I'm sure you can. But a fire fight in public here in Switzerland . . .' Charles Russell shook his head with decision but not because he doubted her competence. She must be very good indeed or they wouldn't have handed her out a gun. They'd have tested her before giving her training, for there was something about a woman with firearms which gave pause to all experienced spymasters.

They drove through a dreary but opulent suburb till they came to Molina's impressive villa. At the lodge Helen stopped though the gate was open. Russell noticed that it opened outwards. Helen switched off the engine and turned to Russell. 'So I'll tell you what I know of the layout. When I climbed up that tree at the side I could see the yard. There were windows looking out on it but I'd guess they will have been servants' bedrooms. And that night when I blundered about and got caught I had lost my sense of direction entirely. But I did look out of one bedroom window and that window overlooked the drive. The door opened onto a corridor, the corridor where I lost my way, and the bedroom where they're keeping Campbell I'm pretty sure is on the same corridor. If that's right then Campbell's bedroom is at the front.'

'Very good observation indeed but only relevant if considering force. In some ways I'm sorry we're not. Drive on.'

They drove through the gate up the drive to the porch

and Russell got down from the car. 'You stay here. On no account be provoked into gunplay, but if anyone acts foolishly, if I don't come out within, say, twenty minutes, there's only one place to go. That's the police. It will blow us all irrevocably, it's the very last thing I want to happen, but I'm no sort of telly serial hero.'

He climbed the undistinguished steps and rang the bell. To the servant who answered he said in fair Spanish: 'I should like to see your master, please.'

'My master is out.'

'Then whoever's in charge.'

He was shown into what was Molina's study and left to wait for a full five minutes. He looked at his watch: time was running against him. But finally a man came in. He said peremptorily, without an attempt at courtesy: 'Your name and business, please. At once.'

'My name is Charles Russell. You may possibly know it.'

The arrogant but wary face changed instantly to naked hatred. 'Charles Russell,' its owner said. 'I have heard of you.' The words were few but their meaning evident. Clark detested Russell for what he stood for, in general for a degenerate world, in particular for a man who propped it.

'I don't think I've had the pleasure of meeting you.'

'And socially you never will.'

'But I fancy your name is Belami Clark.'

Clark took it without moving a muscle. 'That's perfectly correct,' he said.

'It's a pity your master isn't here.' Russell had given up hope of reason but he might still trap Clark into making some slip. And he had taken an instant decision, standing. Rather than leave James Campbell here, in the hands of this dangerous ruthless man, he would blow the whole operation wide open by going to the Swiss police and telling them. This went flatly against a lifetime's discipline, it smelt strongly of the humanist heresy, for what was the life of a single man against the chances of an irredeemable tragedy? They might prosecute Clark but he'd try again. More probably they wouldn't pursue him, they'd hush everything up as Swiss ethos demanded. Back to Square One, Russell looking a fool. But he said again acidly: 'Your master.'

Clark answered this as Russell had thought he would.

'Molina was never my master. Never.'

'Then you've been using him.'

'You will state your business.'

'By all means. I have come for James Campbell.'

'I don't know what you mean.'

Russell sighed. This was an unwelcome reversion to the manner of a routine police questioning. He'd thought better of Belami Clark than that. 'Jack it up,' he said briefly. 'I hate wasting time.'

'Very well, I'll return to your own high level.' It was intended as irony, sounded like loathing. 'James Campbell is here. May I ask what of it?'

'Simply that I want James Campbell.'

'And if you don't get him?'

'I shall go to the police.'

'Rubbish,' Clark said. 'You are bluffing. I call you.'

'I gave you my name. I am not resourceless.'

'In this matter you are in practice resourceless. Any force you can use I can match and will. As for the police, that is idle chatter. No doubt they could embarrass me but they'd do more to you before they

102

reached me. In any case, before they did so James Campbell would not be alive to be taken.'

Charles Russell could accept a defeat. 'Very well,' he said; he walked out of the room. He hadn't a doubt Clark would do what he threatened.

The same servant let him out of the house but on the undistinguished steps he froze suddenly. Helen was still in the car as he'd left her but she was staring at the house intently. When she saw him she made an urgent gesture. He ran to the car.

'What is it?'

'Look.' She was pointing at an upper window.

'I can't see a thing.'

'There was a face at that window.'

'Whose face?'

'It was Campbell's.'

'You're dreaming. He's drugged.'

Helen said stubbornly: 'No, we should wait. I tell you the man was moving too.'

Russell knew that she wasn't a fanciful woman, and something in her manner convinced him. 'If you're right we're going to see some action. I don't know what action but we've got to be ready. Turn the car round and start the engine.'

She did so.

They stared up at the window again in silence and incredibly a face came up again.

'He's trying to pull himself upright. What do we do?'

Charles Russell didn't answer her. The reason was that he didn't know. They could see the man's body now. He was naked. The window began to open slowly.

'Oh God,' Helen said, 'he means to jump.'

'Have we anything to break the fall?'

'Of course we haven't—I'm not a fireman. But if I could get under the drop . . .'

She had started to leave the car but he pulled her back. 'Perhaps I could manage an injured man but hardly a man plus an injured woman. In any case I don't know this car.'

They were both watching Campbell again as he struggled. He was evidently weak and ill. He had a knee across the window sill, trying to heave the rest of his body up to it.

'Ready to move,' Russell said. 'Not much time.'

Campbell had managed to get his body up.

'I think he means to hang by his hands.'

But he didn't; he lost control; he fell.

They were on to him at once, together. 'He's alive,' Helen said. 'I can see him breathing.'

'Alive or dead we've got to move him. I'll take his shoulders and you take his legs.'

Together they bundled him into the car. Helen Monteath let the clutch in fiercely. Behind them there was a sudden uproar, the clamour of angry voices shouting.

'Drive,' Russell said.

'Believe me, I mean to.'

The rear window behind them splintered suddenly. The glass fell around them but left them whole.

'Rifle, I think,' Russell said. 'That's bad.'

'Why worse than a handgun?'

'Longer range. They can reach us right down to the lodge.'

'I see.' She was beating the car to its limits of tolerance, tearing the tidy gravel to pieces as the radial tyres bit into it savagely, but otherwise she was icily cool. He hadn't needed to tell her to weave. She was weaving.

A good one, he thought—oh, very good. A pity the wrong side had had to have her.

Or was it the wrong side? He'd recently wondered.

There was a second crack behind them. They lurched.

'Back tyre,' Helen said.

'Can you hold her?'

'I'll try.'

She'd been driving in third for acceleration but now she changed down smoothly to second. The hotted-up engine was screaming in protest for the speed had slackened hardly at all. Russell looked down what was left of the drive.

'They've got a line to the lodge or maybe a radio.'

'How do you know?'

'A man's shutting the gate but it opens outwards.'

'Right,' Helen said. 'Stand by.'

'For what?'

'I haven't a clue, it's Navy talk. I had a boy friend in the Navy once and a crashing great bore he was at that.'

The man had the gate half shut by now but Helen Monteath drove into it squarely. There was the crunch of smashed headlights, of buckled wings, and for a second the impact slowed them dangerously. A third shot came through the broken rear window. It missed between them but smashed the windscreen. The man on the gate had been swept in a ditch.

Helen asked as she changed back to third: 'Do you think they'll follow?'

'Not here in Switzerland.'

She looked at the dashboard and laughed almost naturally. 'The oil pressure has fallen to zero and the radiator is boiling happily. But I think we can just about make the chalet.'

'Good,' Russell said. 'That's rather good.'

He wasn't to be outdone in nonchalance.

7

At the chalet they put Campbell to bed and Helen
Monteath rang down to the Aqua Club. 'Molina is
coming at once,' she told Russell, 'and he's going to
bring his doctor with him.'

Charles Russell looked at Helen approvingly. 'Then
I'll only be in the way if I stay.'

'Your absence might shorten the explanations. A car
shot to pieces to mention no other.'

'Which you'll naturally handle much better alone.'

'But come back for luncheon and meet Molina.'

'A pleasure I can hardly wait for.'

'I'll ring for a taxi.'

'No, I'll walk.' After any excitement he liked to
unwind and the morning had only confirmed his
impression that Helen Monteath could be wholly
trusted. It was better to leave her to talk to Molina, and
what the doctor would doubtless do for Campbell
would not be advanced by his own attendance.

Molina and the doctor arrived five minutes after
Russell's departure. The doctor went straight upstairs
to Campbell but Molina stayed below with Helen. She
began to explain and he seemed to be listening, but he
gave her a faintly unnerving impression that only a half
of his mind was interested. In some curious way he
knew it all, this was something he had already foreseen,
if not in the details of what had happened in the

certainty of some form of crisis. When she had finished he nodded casually.

'Don't worry, this will not be repeated.'

It wouldn't be, he was thinking privately. He had given Clark seventy-two hours and few were left.

The doctor rejoined them brisk but percipient, as doctors with rich patients needed to be. He had decided over a lifetime of treating them that the rich were a different race with different rules. One was their right to tell what they wished to and its complement that you mustn't ask questions. So he sat down and accepted a drink from Helen but it was to Molina that he addressed himself. His manner was as matter of fact as though he had been discussing the weather.

'Your friend upstairs has no gunshot or stab wounds. I mention this because if he had I'd be obliged to report the matter embarrassingly. As it is all I know or need to know is that I've been called to a case of multiple bruising by another patient I've treated for years. I don't think that bruising was caused by a beating, so again I'm safely within my duties.' He held up a hand. 'No explanations, please—I beg you. It's doubtful if I'd believe a word since your friend is also full of some drug. A barbiturate, I rather fancy, but of course that could have been self-administered. There are people who take more than is good for them and then, shall we say? they fall downstairs.'

'We'll accept your diagnosis happily.' Molina was as bland as butter.

'So speculation is not my business but the condition of a patient is. The bruising is serious though nothing is broken, but I'm worried about the persistent drugging. I've given him something to help to disperse it but what he really needs is rest and quiet. A light supper tonight and no talk whatever. He needs peace to let his own body work for him. I'll come back tomorrow and look again.'

When the doctor had gone Helen said to Molina: 'Will you stay for lunch?'

'I'd very much like to.'

'I've a guest, the man I spoke of before.'

'The man who helped you to rescue Campbell?'

'Colonel Charles Russell.'

'Another agent?'

'I suppose you could call him that if you had to. He's in a very different class from myself.'

'Then he must,' Molina said, 'be worth meeting.' He was normally very sparing of flattery.

'I think you will find him that.'

Molina did. He and Charles Russell were at ease very quickly, each seeing in the other man something to be admired and respected, perhaps something which he lacked himself. Helen had cooked them veal and red cabbage and all of them ate with a happy appetite. There was an unspoken but effective agreement that the events of the morning should not be mentioned, but they talked with an increasing freedom of any other subject of interest. To Russell this seemed in no way strange. He was experienced at reading the signals and had decided after the first five minutes that the reason Molina was keeping silence on a matter which must concern him deeply was that it had also set him a private problem. What was more he had made his decision to cope with it, but until he had carried it out he would rather not talk.

Fair enough, Russell thought, and I don't need to

press him, for I'm sure enough now which side he's on. Not actively on ours, or not yet, but at the lowest Clark has something on him, a hold which he's determined to break. That suits us very well indeed.

So the table talk flowed on urbanely, neither the gossip which Molina despised nor the fashionable and mostly foolish politics which exacerbated Russell wickedly. To Charles Russell Molina was not a failure but a man who had fought on a dangerous battlefield and emerged from it if not with victory at least with very handsome spoils. Molina simply thought of Russell that here was a man you could talk to sensibly, a man with an evident sense of reality. This relationship once established silently Charles Russell asked a forthright question which even half an hour before he would have considered a clumsy and fruitless blunder.

'You've lived here off and on, I gather. Have you ever heard of something called Lenterheims?'

'Of course I have. They make pharmaceuticals.'

'Anything else?'

'I've heard they've also branched out into fertilizers.' Molina raised a shrewd eyebrow at Russell. 'If you're interested why don't we go there? There are open days on Sundays and Fridays, at three o'clock, and to-day is a Sunday. A public relations affair but they let you in. Normally the place is a fortress.'

'A fortress?' Russell repeated.

'Not literally but they're strict about strangers. Passes and all the rest of it. Guards. But on the open days they show you some of it, how clean it is, how modern, how Swissbiss, and afterwards there's sweet cakes and coffee.'

'You've done it, then?'

'Several years ago. Not a reason not to go again.'

Helen stayed behind to watch Campbell but the men drove to Lenterheims' office block, pulling up before an impressive monster in the manner of the 1950s. There was a great deal of glass and irrelevant ornament. A coach from the town drew up behind them, disgorging a modest cargo of visitors, and a man who was clearly the guide got out with them. Russell and Molina joined them and the guide made a little speech of welcome. Then the splendid but hideous doors were thrown open and the guide began his practised patter.

He led them first to the pharmaceuticals, talking fluently in French and German, and at pre-arranged points he halted briefly while a tape played his message in other tongues. This message was always the same and emphatic: this was drug-making at its most modern—responsible. Not all of them would have technical knowledge but they could see for themselves the scrupulous cleanliness, the high standard of all research and control. These spoke for themselves in any language. There was one sly dig but only one: when Lenterheims spoke of testing they meant it; they'd never marketed a drug of disaster, particularly not a drug for women.

Charles Russell let the patter flow over him. He seldom took drugs, not even aspirin, and was happily blessed with regular bowels, but he looked down the long air-conditioned laboratories with an interest unconnected with medicines. Most of them ran east to west and Russell remembered his view through binoculars. The high-security block, the wire, the guards, would lie to the north of these soulless caverns.

Which had windows facing north but all were

111

screened. Those facing south were not.

. . . Perhaps nothing.

They climbed into the coach again, driving maybe half a mile to the different world of commercial fertilizers. Russell had no industrial knowledge and this plant told him nothing beyond the obvious, that it was new and very efficient indeed. It was screened from the high-security block by rising ground and a belt of conifers which to Russell's eyes looked newly planted, but on the way there had been a sudden glimpse of wire fencing and two men in uniform. It hadn't lasted for more than a matter of seconds but the driver had seemed to accelerate sharply and returning to their cakes and coffee there was the same brief sighting, the short burst of speed.

At the back of the coach someone pointed a finger, calling to the guide: 'What's that?'

The guide had had this question before and his answer had been prepared with some care. 'I'm sorry I can't show you that just yet, it's one of the company's little experiments. Naturally we make them to keep ahead and naturally we have commercial competitors.' The guide's manner was slick as a good mayonnaise. 'Suppose one of you gentlemen or even a lady . . .' He laughed at this feeble joke. No one else did. They were mostly from German-speaking Switzerland. . . . Pompous gentleman slips on banana skin, breaks his leg. Roars of satisfied and happy laughter. Anything less left their faces solemn masks.

At the Bleiner Molina dropped Russell politely. He went up to his room and rang the bell. It was answered by the middle-aged waiter who Helen had told him was also their radio link. He worked on short wave to a house in Bonn and afterwards it went diplomatic.

'A large whisky and soda, please.'

'Of course. But first I have a message.'

'Yes?'

'The sender would like your reassurance on a matter which both of you once discussed.'

'Is that a literal translation?'

'Certainly.'

'Then make it a very large whisky indeed.'

Charles Russell was a little put out. He knew that the General was under pressure—he'd apologized for the cliché 'hawks'—but he didn't know he'd been given a time limit, far less that, allowing for different times, several of those ten days had slipped away. But even if he had known these facts he would still have thought 'reassurance' unreasonable. In the Security Executive his tasks had been simple, or simple enough to define with conviction. You found out about something and if possible stopped it; you would go to very great lengths to do that, bending the law as a matter of course and all too often breaking it secretly. If you were caught then you carried the can. But his present commission was outside experience. He hadn't even been asked to establish that A was in reality B, but that A, which the General believed existed and which Russell had now agreed might do so, wasn't A at all but in one sense A's noumen, not a plan to carry out A in deed but to give the impression that that was the danger and so frighten men with whose fears Russell sympathized into action which could mean mutual destruction.

Not a matter where 'reassurance' was quite the word. Nevertheless he must send an answer and he began to write it down in rough.

1. *Nothing has happened to disprove the hypothesis that our enemy's plan is one of Deception. Equally I have seen no hard evidence of making nuclear weapons in secret.*
2. *But I have visited Lenterheims as you suggested in London and there is a heavily guarded section there where visitors are not admitted.*
3. *Campbell may be able to throw some light on that if he is well enough to talk tomorrow. As you will doubtless have heard from Mrs Monteath he has been recovered and is now available.*

Charles Russell read this through with care. It would have to be tidied up of course, but it was accurate on such facts as were known. He reflected, then added another paragraph, for Lenterheims' name still tantalized memory. Something to do with the war, he fancied.

4. *Kindly fill me in on Lenterheims' background. Activities, if any, in 1939-45 war could be relevant.*

He was boiling this message down when he laughed. His humour was entirely his own, ironical and a trifle pungent, and it struck him as something more than amusing that after half a lifetime spent fighting communism he should now be sending reports and questions to a man who had once been his principal enemy. In theory, that is, though never personally. He had always got on very well with the General. But the world. had changed though *realpolitik* hadn't. Yesterday's enemy, now his collaborator.

Amusing? he thought. It was surely that, but it was

114

also in its way illustrative. It showed how his own mind had changed with time. When Helen Monteath had asked him for work he had sent her to the General instead. He had known that the action was wildly irregular but at the time it had seemed to him perfectly logical. At the time—a bare three years ago. When he'd often and sometimes with secret success co-operated with the official enemy but when he wouldn't have even dreamed in a nightmare of accepting his direct commission. Had he swung right round without even suspecting it, did he now think of orthodox disciplined communism as the saviour of a decadent Europe? No, not quite that, it was much more negative. . . . 'Communism is a disease of defeated nations.' Now who had said that? He couldn't remember. Unimportant since it wasn't true. The disease of a degenerate nation was something called egalitarian socialism. Which hardline communism destroyed at sight. Russell, at the lowest, mistrusted it. So perhaps he could find himself not guilty of the shameful sin of thinking loosely. This message he was writing the General—that wasn't an illogical act.

He compressed it but left in all four paragraphs. He would give it to the waiter at dinner. The channel now had a listener for every twenty-four hours of the day and night so Russell could hope for an answer by midnight.

While he picked at the Bleiner's terrible dinner Molina and Helen were talking business. Over their own and better meal Helen said quietly: 'About tomorrow.'

'You mean about talking to Campbell? We need to.'

If she noticed the plural she made no comment. Without anything said and far less formalized Molina had joined herself and Russell. 'The doctor is coming tomorrow morning but I've been up to our friend and he looks much better. With luck we should be able to talk to him. Not for long, I dare say, but enough to help us.' Her voice changed from a modest optimism to one with an undertone of unease. 'Meanwhile there's still the question of Clark. You don't think he'll do anything foolish like trying to recover Campbell from here?'

'It's conceivable but I think it unlikely. I sincerely hope you didn't notice him but one of my men is now watching this house. Incidentally I'm sorry I can't stay the night.'

He was pleased that her disappointment was evident and began to explain his reason shortly. 'After that assault in my house I gave Belami Clark three days to leave it. That was at nine o'clock in the morning and at nine tomorrow his time expires. I'm punctilious about matters of that sort and inclined to oversleep in the morning. So I mean to be at home to enforce the deadline.'

Helen didn't reply but hid her doubts. As an agent she had more than one but Molina would hardly think as she did. . . . Throw out Clark? A very natural reaction. But he'd merely go underground elsewhere, leaving Russell and herself to find him. And she suspected there must be others too, if not actually yet arrived in Neuwald almost certainly on their way to do so. These would have to be flushed and that might not be easy if the brains and the driving force were also in hiding.

But she said nothing of this to Molina—she dare not. He had joined them, they had interests in common, but she couldn't expect him to share her doubts. Instead she said: 'Do you have a gun? I could lend you one.'

He gave her an almost sly smile. 'No gun. The weapon of my blood is the knife but I haven't had to use one for years. With a gun I should be perfectly useless.' He rose from the table. 'So *hasta mañana*. Try and get a good night's rest.'

'I rather doubt it.'

'I take that as a charming compliment. By the way, my man outside *is* armed, but I very much doubt if Clark will try anything.'

Nor did he; he wasn't fit to do so. For he was shattered again as he always was when the Black Dog chose to ride on his shoulder. It had been a variant of the familiar nightmare, this time not a recollection of fact but an agonizing fantasy. Worse.

For this time he hadn't been out on the road watching disaster's debris flow past him, the burned and the maimed and the terrified children, but standing helpless in his own small home. He saw it with an appalling clarity, the neatness, the more than Dutch sense of cleanliness. It had been sparsely furnished, the living-room tiny, made tolerable to a European by the Japanese respect for space. In the rush hour their transport was dangerously crowded, the fight for a place on it one without quarter, but put him in his home or his office and no Japanese would ever walk into you. In this absurd little room there'd been space for all five of them.

And now it was a blistering furnace, his children with their clothes in flames, his Japanese wife, herself a torch, trying desperately to beat them out. The cries and the oven smell of burning flesh, a Gehenna outside the unglazed window, the feel of some cosmic disaster, of impotence. For as always in nightmares he couldn't move. Miraculously untouched himself he'd had to stand there and watch till released by awakening.

This time he woke at three o'clock, shivering. He changed his pyjamas again and took a shower. What was left of the night he spent in chain smoking. He was shaken but also confirmed in purpose.

Molina knew nothing of this next morning when he sent for Clark at nine o'clock. He had expected excuses and possibly protest but not what he in fact received. He began as he had put it to Helen, moderately but perfectly firmly.

'I had hoped that I wouldn't have to send for you but since you've forced my hand I'm obliged to do so. I gave you three days to leave this house and that time is up this morning. Now.'

'That's perfectly correct,' Clark said. He had sat without an invitation. He had never had any intention of going and this morning he was in no mood for the courtesies. He had thought it before and he thought it again: this degenerate little ex-dictator had no idea what he'd let himself in for.

'Then I insist that you comply at once.'

'Don't be silly,' Clark said, 'you hold no hand.' He knew nothing of Russell's talk with Helen when they'd decided they dare not invoke the police but in substance he repeated Charles Russell. 'For what can you do? The police? But of course not. The police might help you or maybe they wouldn't, but the police have sharp noses and would certainly use them. The moment they picked up even a hint of what's really been going on in this house your residence permit would be quietly withdrawn. You'd be out of this country, my friend, and you wouldn't like it. You are happy here, you've a hobby, a mistress. It's a fine life here for a very rich man, you're enjoying your spoils and you won't forgo them.'

Molina kept his temper admirably. 'I think you misread the situation. I had never considered the police. No indeed.'

'Then you're thinking of those two men of yours? You think that it's myself and a Dutchman against a couple of your native thugs? Then it's you who are misreading badly. For it isn't two against two or knives against pistols. I dispose of a good deal more than even odds.'

In the silence Belami Clark checked his statement. He had called up six men from their hides in Germany and four had already arrived in Neuwald—two of the three Spanish anarchists, the Belgian and one Japanese. The Japanese was the best of all of them, the only one he considered an equal. All four had discreetly gone to ground but all had made contact with Belami Clark.

Belami Clark allowed a smile. He could well afford to call down Molina.

He did so. He did it without tact or grace for he wasn't in the mood for either. His dislike of this miserable ex-dictator had swollen into a bitter contempt. He would spare him no humiliation.

'Well?' he said dangerously.

'Far from well. But you will realize that I have allies too.'

'You mean your newly found English friends? Forget them. A man in his sixties, a woman agent. The former is too old for violence and the latter has trapped you into her bed.' He rose before Molina could answer. 'So I hope you understand me clearly. I shall leave this house when it suits me to do so and that may not be for several days.' He walked to the door but turned at it sharply. He had an exit line and he meant to deliver it. It was an insult but he was well past caring.

'Meanwhile I'd prefer to eat alone.'

Belami Clark had no idea of it but with this sentence he had committed suicide.

Charles Russell had also woken at three but not from a nightmare—from a knock on his door. The waiter gave him a sheet of paper. 'Too long to take orally.'

'Thank you. I'll read it.'

FOR RUSSELL FROM OLD ACQUAINTANCE. BEGINS.

1. *Lenterheims, though a company registered in Switzerland, is almost certainly German controlled. You inquire about its position in the 1939-45 war. Switzerland being neutral Lenterheims was free to trade with the Reich and did so with enthusiasm. We find this deplorable but it wasn't illegal.*
2. *But its assets in the United Kingdom were taken under control by the Custodian of Enemy Property. He was entitled to do this under the Trading with the Enemy Act, 1939 (as amended) provided he could show that real control was German and therefore 'enemy'. Lenterheims went to the Courts on the matter of fact and won in the court of first instance. The Custodian appealed and was upheld in the Court of Appeal by a majority judgment.*

*3. We have no reason to suppose that effective control
has changed since 1945. On the contrary it may well
have increased.*

Charles Russell in his bed sighed deeply for he
relished this message in no way whatever. There'd been
a tacit but lively understanding between himself and his
friend the Colonel-General that what existed as their
now mutual problem was a plan to frighten the
General's hawks into action which might destroy the
West. The General didn't want that, nor Russell, but
both had to do the near impossible, to prove that
something which looked very much for real was in fact
a gigantic but organized sham. And now it was more
than an organized sham, it was a sham with a very good
mind behind it. Disordered perhaps but still very good.
For Lenterheims was German controlled, so whatever
the next development be Charles Russell was sure it
would centre on Lenterheims. And if Lenterheims was
really German what Russian would ever believe it was
innocent? It might be white as a detergent plug but even
the Russian doves would turn hawk.

This was very well considered planning. Credibility
had increased uncomfortably.

8

When Russell arrived at the chalet next morning Molina was already there and the doctor had made his promised call. Helen gave Russell his morning coffee and Molina greeted the visitor pleasantly, not too casually as the old friend he wasn't but secure in the knowledge of common interests. 'Campbell seems very much better,' he said, 'and the doctor says he can talk a little. Not to tire him, though. Say twenty minutes.'

They went upstairs to Campbell's room. He was propped up on pillows but looking robuster. Helen noticed that he had eaten his breakfast, for she had gone to some trouble to find him oatmeal. He said with a typically Scots understatement: 'I'm sorry to have been such a nuisance. I wish I could repay you.'

'You can.' Charles Russell, receiving permission, lit a cigar. 'You remember our talk in London? The one at the club?'

'Very well indeed. I must now renege on it. As I remember I said that it simply wasn't on to snatch any form of nuclear material.' He added with his normal dourness: 'I hedged my bet by saying "in practice", but clearly if you can snatch a man you can snatch almost anything else you fancy, though I still can't work out why they picked on me.'

'I gave you perhaps a quarter answer when I talked about a friend of mine with a very serious worry indeed.' Since his words had been succinct Russell used them again. 'He doesn't fear making a Bomb in secret; he fears the appearance that that might be happening. That appearance would have to be built up carefully, and kidnapping a nuclear scientist would fit in with that as an opening gambit.'

James Campbell considered this and then nodded. 'That meshes with your unnamed friend's fear though it's still, as you'll have to admit, a hypothesis. And in any case why bring me to Neuwald?'

'Have you ever heard of Lenterheims? They operate from here, you know.'

'Pharmaceuticals? And recently fertilizers?'

'And possibly something else,' Russell said.

He began to bring Campbell up to date, thinking as he recited the facts that there was precious little firm to lean on, wishing that he himself had possessed some shred of technical knowledge to help him. There must have been some clue at Lenterheims which to a man with that knowledge would have opened the door.

Campbell at the end said: 'Not proven. Suspicion enough, which according to you is what some people are trying to build up, but the evidence that the House of Lenterheims is playing with anything nuclear is pretty thin.'

Molina said unexpectedly: 'No.' He had remembered the talk he had had with his doctor. It had significance now and he began to repeat it: that in certain matters the doctor was helpless, that men were all human and so sometimes careless. A phrase came back to him verbatim. ' "That man on the crutches was only careless but he's the third case I've had this year. All will die." '

He spoke into an increasing interest and when he had

123

finished James Campbell frowned. 'Still not conclusive but much more suspicious. Radiation poisoning. So——'

'So they're making a weapon.' It was Helen Monteath.

'No, not at all. That's extremely improbable.' James Campbell was a little sharp. He knew nothing of women since he didn't much care for them and he resented that one should have interrupted the cautious processes of his deliberate mind.

But Helen was unabashed. 'Then what?' She had lived with a Scot and knew their virtues. Also something of their evident defects of which one was a certain mental rigidity. They hated to miss a step on a ladder even when other men skipped it quite safely.

'I was coming to that, given time,' he said. He turned back to Russell a trifle too noticeably. 'Going back to our talk in London, then, I explained that any nuclear power plant meant plutonium in considerable quantity. And plutonium must be recycled back if it isn't to be used for a weapon.'

Whilst the others absorbed what to Campbell was obvious James Campbell himself reflected grimly. His thoughts were gloomy to the edge of hopelessness; he could see the world's danger but knew no remedy. He didn't believe that the major Powers would destroy each other except maybe by accident but the smaller were far less secure and predictable. Suppose some preposterous stateling in Africa demanded the gift of a nuclear power plant. The Great Powers would oppose the proposal·discreetly but imagine the fuss on the Lunatic Left, the talk of the Rich Man's Club of the West, the accusations of selfish deprivation. Why shouldn't these men have what others had, Israel and India to offer examples? And once he had nuclear power and pluotonium how long before some tribal atavist threw a crude and distressingly dirty Bomb at some neighbour he believed had slighted him?

James Campbell sighed for he knew no answer.

Charles Russell brought him back to reality. 'How far have we come from the original guesswork?'

'I still don't accept that Lenterheims can be making a weapon or anything like it. For one thing the Swiss would never permit it. But I do accept that on all the evidence there's a case they may be engaged in recycling.' It was lucid if a trifle ponderous. 'There's nothing illegal in that whatever. It's done all over the world and commercially, except in the United States where Congress has kept it away from big business.'

Helen Monteath looked at Campbelll carefully. He was tiring but he hadn't yet finished and an important question was still to come. Charles Russell said:

'Very well—recycling. Then where does the plutonium come from?'

'We discussed that aspect before—it comes from Germany. Germany is ahead of the rest of us in the third generation of nuclear power stations. Germany is awash with plutonium, maybe more than she can handle herself, and if that is correct there'd be nothing improper in sending to a country like Switzerland any surplus beyond her own capacity. There are advantages in being professionally neutral.'

'Then the recycled product goes back to Germany?'

'Almost certainly it does just that.'

Helen rose for she'd been quietly timing them and they were over the doctor's twenty minutes. She expertly settled Campbell to rest again and the three of them went downstairs to the living-room. Helen poured two gin and tonics but gave Russell a sherry without inquiry.

He was showing an unusual excitement. 'There's one uncertainty we ought to eliminate before we accept the recycling theory.' He turned to Molina. 'Will you please ring your doctor? I want to know about medical isotopes, the radioactive affairs which are used diagnostically. Lenterheims are still pharmaceuticals and that might be an explanation.'

Molina returned in five minutes, satisfied. 'You can eliminate them,' he said with some emphasis. 'There are several and very effective ways of making a medical isotope active without using any form of plutonium, and even if you did it that way the quantity would be infinitesimal. You certainly wouldn't need a new plant.'

Charles Russell accepted another sherry; he looked at the other two, stroking his chin. 'Then we're agreed that it's recycling?'

Two nods.

'Plutonium which comes from Germany?'

Helen said: 'Yes, it sounds like that.'

'Then how does that plutonium get here?'

There was a longish silence which Molina broke. 'Perhaps I could make a guess at that. It happened a year ago, though.'

'Never mind.'

'I suspect it comes across the lake on a ferry they don't show in the timetable.' He finished his drink: Helen gave him another. 'I had a friend on the other side of the water.' He smiled at Helen, quite unembarrassed. 'Of course I didn't know you then or I

126

wouldn't have caught the chill I did. Anyway I put the car on the ferry since I was taking the lady out to dinner, and one thing led to another the way it does. In the event I missed the last ferry back and there was a reason I couldn't return to the lady. I was stranded on the German side.'

'Awkward,' Charles Russell said.

'It was. But I did get back and I'll tell you how. You see, there was another ferry, not scheduled and it sailed in the small hours. I'd suspected there must be something like that when I got down to the quay and saw the *cortège*. No, *cortège* isn't the word: I mean convoy. A military convoy at that. There was an armoured vehicle, a scout car, I think, and two lorry loads of German infantry in what looked to me like battle order.'

'Anything else?'

'I was coming to that. There was a fourth vehicle like a prison van, square windowless sides and a grille for the drivers. It never moved without the infantrymen, three or four on each side and looking all ways. Weapons at the ready. A guard.'

'And they allowed you to see all this?'

'Not exactly. The man I had bribed to slip me on—not a soldier of course but a man from the ferry, and a good deal of money it took to persuade him—this man locked me up in the ordinary waiting-room. But there was a window and lights outside. I could see something.'

'You saw a remarkable lot. Go on.'

'They left the armoured car behind but they drove the prison van on the ferry with maybe a dozen soldiers still guarding it. Then my man came back with a pair of sea

127

boots, a duffle coat and a tatty cap. In those he slipped me onto the ferry but of course I had to leave the car. He took me straight down to a cabin and left me. I wasn't to move or he'd have me arrested, when he'd naturally deny all knowledge. If they found me, he said, they might even shoot me and drop me in deep water, weighted.'

'Quite possibly true. But you went ahead?'

'I didn't fancy a night in a strange hotel and anyway I was now committed.'

Charles Russell laughed; he admired this panache. 'What happened then?'

'Not much I could see. The cabin's porthole was blackened but half-way I could hear things. You know the international frontier in theory runs down that dim lake's centre, and the Swiss being what a strange God made them I was pretty sure that armed German soldiers would never be allowed on their side. And sure enough about half-way across the ferry hove to and things started to happen. I could hear a launch come alongside the ferry and men clanking up a gangway in boots. Some shouting in Swiss German, then a wait. Then more orders, this time in proper German, afterwards more boots on the gangway. Changing the guard, I thought. I was right. For I could hear the launch start her engine again, and though of course I couldn't be sure I think the direction she took was Germany.'

'How did you get off the ferry?'

'There were other seamen—I went along with them. It was dark still and nobody asked me questions, but Swiss gendarmes were driving the prison van.'

'You're a very cool hand,' Charles Russell said.

Molina looked surprised. 'I am? But remember I'd paid an expensive passage and I've always hated wasting money.' He and Charles Russell exchanged cigars. 'Now what do you make of all that?'

'Enough. They bring it across the lake all right.' Charles Russell smoked half an inch of his fine cigar. 'Do you remember what day of the week this was?'

'It was in the small hours of a Tuesday morning. I remember because as I left the ferry one of the seamen wished me good night. As I told you, nobody challenged me but this seaman said something like: 'See you on Thursday. Forty-eight hours to catch up on our sleep.'

'So Tuesdays and Thursdays are running across days?'

'Perhaps others too but those for sure.'

'And we're talking on a Monday morning.'

'I follow your thoughts. Also I have a cabin cruiser which I keep at one of the private moorings. She's seldom used but I keep her fuelled.'

'If they take this small hours run of theirs as seriously as your story suggests there'll be water police watching the moorings closely. They're not going to let us go out at night.'

'Saving your presence I'd thought of that.' Molina turned to Helen. 'Have you a map?'

She had a plan at the back of a guidebook.

'So.' Molina pointed with Russell's cigar. 'There— three or four miles to the north of Neuwald. There's an empty house with a usable jetty. I'll take the cruiser in the afternoon and I'll wait for you at midnight. Agreed?'

Charles Russell said: 'Thank you.' Molina nodded. Helen Monteath said: 'I'm coming too.'

'Oh no, you're not.'

'Just try and stop me. I'm handy in a boat, what's more. We had one on the loch in Scotland.'

Russell said mildly: 'I'd like to have her. She has other talents than handling boats.

Clark's confidence had not been dented by the setback of James Campbell's rescue. It would doubtless have been more dramatic if his body had been found in the lake as planned, but against this could be set Charles Russell's arrival and the fact that he'd thought a rescue necessary. Charles Russell was an undoubted nuisance and that woman of his, now Molina's mistress, had proved that she was well trained and competent, but an attempt to eliminate either or both would be very ill timed and maybe disastrous. Whoever employed them would promptly replace them and probably reinforce as well. Which Belami Clark didn't wish to happen. A man in his sixties, a single woman, were something which he felt sure he could cope with; he didn't desire that this dull little town should be swarming with armed and ruthless enemies.

Similarly as regards Molina. That too had not gone quite to plan. Molina had tried to throw him out, something Clark hadn't foreseen or expected, but he'd known how to call that bluff and had done so. It suited him well to stay on at Molina's where he could move freely and needn't go underground. The villa was part of his well thought out cover, as was his apparent keenness on daily waterskiing. In fact the pastime bored him cruelly.

But these two setbacks apart and neither fatal everything was going smoothly. He had four men in a deserted house with a radio link which he used very sparingly. And the first of the Japanese was amongst them, the only man he really trusted, the only other who knew the essential twist. The rest were the daily labourers, the necessary hired hands of violence.

He wondered whether he'd mistimed sending for them. The action was still several days away and they'd be spending most of their time playing cards. But no, he had had to give them time, time to practise in the boat at night. Feeding and arming a private army had proved a surprisingly costly business. So had been hired aeroplanes and broken-down pilots to take a risk in them, but the biggest cost of all had been information. Clark had a man in a German power station who gave him the days of consignments to Lenterheims—far more important, what each really was. But this man was no sympathizer, simply rapacious.

But he'd still had enough to acquire a boat—ten per cent for a week on approval and the rest when he found if the boat really suited him. He allowed a sour smile at the thought of that. A thin chance that rich pig whom he'd bought the boat from had of seeing the rest of his money. Ever. For in less than a week it would all be over, when the boat could be shot to pieces or sunk but he and his men safely out of the country.

Or if anything went wrong they'd be dead. The proviso did not disturb his reflections. Human life was of no importance whatever.

He began to consider his men individually for in the last resort he was helpless without them. Apart from the Japanese he thought little of them. They'd be practising at night as he'd told them but by day they'd be lounging about and gambling. Nothing could be worse for morale. Clark would have made a fine commander of any body of troops on active service, on the principle, established by others, that the soldier doing nothing was doing wrong. So he couldn't afford that morale should deteriorate. The two Spaniards neither had discipline nor were amenable to an attempt to enforce it. They were desperate and up to a point brave men but had the volatility of their Latin blood. And the Belgian Clark mistrusted entirely. He was a spoiled intellectual in love with violence, a romantic attachment and therefore suspect. Only the Japanese was reliable. He'd find something to keep himself fit and interested, and he'd do what he could to control the others.

This decided Clark looked at his watch: it was four o' clock. He intended to go and waterski. Molina mostly waterskied at teatime, and if he saw Clark at the Aqua Club Molina would think it another impertinence. Indeed it would be another insult.

Clark laughed without humour; he didn't possess it. But he could analyse his own feelings accurately. Once he'd mistrusted Molina; he'd thought him soft. Then he had learnt to despise and now he hated.

What he didn't consider and finally broke him was that the emotion might be ardently mutual.

9

Molina cast off the cabin cruiser, turning her bows north-west up the coast. She was a solidly built affair sleeping four and she'd been slow as the old cow she looked till Molina had put in a modern engine. Normally he took a man with him, for the lake which looked an amateur's paradise could be treacherous and sometimes worse, but on this trip he would have to manage alone though he knew that he wasn't much of a sailor. If Helen was really handy in boats he'd be pleased enough to have her around, especially if the afternoon haze turned to mist as it sometimes did in the summer. Meanwhile he'd reach the pier and their rendezvous by hugging the coast and playing it safe. In fact this course was far from safe since there were shoals and in places hidden rocks, and a waterguard watched his progress anxiously. But the God whom he nominally worshipped was with him and soon he was out of the dangerous water. He'd have several hours to wait at the pier till the midnight they had agreed to meet but Molina was looking forward to waiting. There was food in the cabin cruiser's galley and a good radio which he'd listen to peacefully. After midnight there would be a moon and an evening on the enchanted water would be a pleasant relief from events which had troubled him.

So he set his course and chugged along happily. His

modern engine would drive the sturdy old craft at a speed which was rather more than respectable but for the moment he was content enough to loiter along and enjoy the outing. His mooring was half a mile south of the Aqua Club and he gave this a wider than usual berth to avoid any danger of hitting a waterskier. There were only two out in the open water and one of them Molina recognized. Belami Clark was getting better. He wasn't yet good but was somewhere near competence; he fell less often and when he did he remounted more smoothly and tried again. Charles Russell had called Molina cool but Molina thought Belami Clark much cooler. He had called Molina's hand contemptuously, he was still in his house with that tedious Dutchman, and here he was amusing himself as though he were an honoured guest.

Belami Clark would pay for that, but the time wasn't ripe and patience earned dividends.

Molina went back to attending the boat, watching the undistinguished coastline. For waterskiing this lake was ideal but as scenery it was simply banal. Further inland were woods and hills but the shore was mostly depressing marsh where the wild birds had been slaughtered remorselessly. The haze was increasing but it wasn't yet mist and Molina motored placidly on.

But when the pier came in sight he stopped the boat suddenly. There was another cabin cruiser busy loading at the little jetty. Four men were climbing in with an air of purpose. Molina dropped anchor and put out a fishing rod. He hadn't the smallest intention of fishing but the rod might be a credible reason for the presence of a second vessel. But in fact the four men showed no interest in his. They put out towards deep water deliberately and in fifteen minutes were lost in the haze. Equally, Molina reckoned, they wouldn't be able to see his next move.

Which was to pull up his anchor and motor on. He tied a line to the jetty and walked along it, up a path to the house he had heard was deserted. Risky, but he'd decided to chance it. If they'd left a fifth man on watch he'd had it.

And it wasn't deserted—very far from it. Nor was another man on watch. He saw collapsible beds, a table, some chairs, and an icebox with a supply of food. A paperback novel in very poor Spanish and a newspaper in an alien script. Molina had counted four men in the boat and now he could count four unmade beds.

He began a more careful search, humming softly. The room downstairs told him nothing more, but he climbed the uncarpeted stairs with confidence. Upstairs there was a sort of workroom, tools of a sort he had never seen and a radio on a folding table. Molina, who knew something of radios, went up to it and examined it carefully. . . . Short wave and range perhaps ten miles. He wondered who held its twin. That Clark?

He decided that it was more than possible—this affair was beginning to form a shape. Charles Russell hadn't yet been explicit but had accepted that something excessively dangerous was coming across this lake twice weekly, and that something could be a tempting target to the sort of man Clark had shown he was. But he could hardly be planning to act with two men, himself and that uncivilized Dutchman, so if these others were not his reinforcements it was difficult to suggest who they were. And had he not mentioned other resources when Molina had fruitlessly tried to eject him? One thing would clinch it and Molina must find it.

He found them in a cupboard, carefully crated but they'd been newly opened. There were machine pistols and an H.V. rifle, and something Molina wasn't sure about. It was a launcher and a box of rockets. The missiles were eighteen inches long and Molina guessed that a steady infantryman could hole anything with them but heavy battle tanks.

Charles Russell would be more than interested.

Molina went back to his cruiser and cast her off. He had had to change his plan but not fatally. The second boat could come back at any time and there was still two hours of diminishing daylight. He was confident that with his modern engine he'd have the legs on the other boat more than comfortably, so he needn't lie off the jetty so far that Charles Russell and Helen would fail to see him. He'd give himself a hundred yards and if the others came back and challenged he'd run for it. Charles Russell was cautious and much too experienced to come through a house he'd been *told* was deserted; he'd come to the jetty across the garden, when Molina would either be there within hailing, in which case they'd proceed with the evening, or else he would have been driven off. But he wouldn't have betrayed his friends by foolishly tying up to the pier where even in the dark he'd be seen if the others returned before Russell's arrival.

So he stationed himself at a hundred yards, still visible as the evening lengthened, but equally able to see the jetty or to hear Charles Russell's call if he made one. He decided not to risk his radio but he cooked himself a tolerable meal. Then he smoked till the real dark came and midnight. The other boat had not returned.

And at midnight he saw a light on the jetty. It went out at once as he started his motor, and he worked his way in with a proper caution. Russell and Helen were standing motionless. The moon was still unborn in its womb but Molina could make out their outlines. He called to Russell: 'Did you come through the garden?'

'Of course we did—the house may have squatters.' Russell began to help Helen down. 'But why do you ask?'

'There aren't any squatters but there are men camping there. Also they have a boat like this one and they've taken it out on the lake. All four of them.'

'How do you know?'

'As for the boat I saw them take her. They haven't come back which is just as well. As for the house I went up and looked at it.'

Russell started to speak but bit it off. Instead he asked Molina politely: 'Anything interesting?'

Molina told him what he had seen. Charles Russell didn't comment; he thought. Skipping inessentials he said: 'It won't be the real thing tonight—that's clear since they've left their weapons behind them. They'll be doing what we intended to do, which was to take a look at how it all worked. We know that the stuff comes across this lake in the small hours of a Tuesday and Thursday. It is safe to assume that they know that too, for though there'll be high security, at any rate on the German side, total secrecy would be almost impossible. As instance the fact that you found out by accident. Our friends will have better sources than that, either from German sympathizers or quite possibly by simply buying it. And if your're right about changing the guard half-way over, from competent German infantry to Swiss gendarmes I'd prefer not to grade, they will want

137

to know how that's done and where. That, if I'm right, is the vulnerable point, and they'll need to see how things work in practice. So for the matter of that do we.' For Russell it had been quite a speech. He drew a long breath but used only a little 'Let's go,' he said. 'We'll stick to our plan.'

'With that other boat out there?' Helen asked. 'The fact there were heavy arms in a cupboard is no guarantee that they don't carry light ones.'

Molina grinned. 'I'm faster than that lot. If anything happens we'll leave in a hurry.'

Russell nodded approvingly—foolish risks were for children. 'Eminently sane and sensible—I was going to make the same suggestion. So since that's agreed we'll be on our way.'

They slipped away into the silent lake. There wasn't a breath of air to stir it and the mist lay in unpredictable patches. In some places it was almost a fog, in others it was almost clear, and in these the moon striped the water vividly. Their bow wave and wake were both sedate, for they were motoring quietly, keeping the noise down. Helen had taken the wheel without protest.

They'd been going for perhaps an hour when Russell held his hand up. Helen stopped.

'About half-way across, would you say?'

'More or less.' They were all of them searching the darkness. Nothing.

Charles Russell turned to Molina beside him. 'When you bribed your way on that ferry that night did you notice if she was showing lights?'

'There was one in my cabin. That's all I know.'

'They would hardly risk it with nothing at all. If they ran down some wretched fishing-boat there'd be all hell to pay, especially in Switzerland. They won't be blazing about like a river gin palace but look out for her navigation lights. Listen.'

The four men in the other cruiser were doing the same. In the middle of the lake it was clearer, but there were pockets of mist and between the two boats a belt of what was almost fog. They were barely half a mile apart but neither had seen the other or heard her.

The men from the villa saw the third vessel first, not the ferry which was still invisible but the launch with the gendarmes coming from Switzerland. She was lighted and making a good deal of noise. The Belgian, who had once owned a yacht, was commanding the cabin cruiser reluctantly. He had stopped his engine but now started it noisily. Helen looked at Russell inquiringly.

'Go slow ahead and see what happens.'

The two cabin cruisers were now converging, though neither yet had the least idea of it. The other reacted first when they sighted. Both were out in the clear, fully free of the fog belt. The ferry too was visible now, anchored and showing her Red and Green. The gendarmes' launch was closing up on her. The ferry which had lowered a gangway suddenly put all her lights on. The gendarmes' launch drew alongside and stopped. Men began to climb the gangway.

Helen asked Russell: 'What now?'

'Just watch.'

'And that lot?' She pointed.

'Just let them watch too.'

But the Belgian had begun to panic. He said to the Japanese: 'I don't like it.'

'They're probably police.'

'Why should they be police? There are gendarmes in that launch already.'

'Then move closer and we'll have a look.'

'I don't like it,' the Belgian said again.

The Japanese shrugged; he drew a pistol. The Belgian began to move: Russell saw him. To Helen he said: 'Keep moving steadily.'

When he was within hailing distance the Japanese stood up and shouted.

'Who are you?'

. . . Not an intelligent question.

Russell looked at the four in the boat through glasses. At twenty-five yards in the ferry's lights he could see their faces with very fair clarity. The man at the wheel was a north European and two others had a Latin look. The fourth was an oriental and angry, and Russell had very good reason indeed to be wary of angry orientals. Particularly when they had pistols and he had not.

Russell, who had been watching the pistol, called unexpectedly: 'Get down.'

They all dropped.

The shot whipped across the open cockpit. Helen half rose, took the wheel with one hand. With the other she opened the throttle, accelerated. She was steering across the other's stern. From the floorboards Russell asked mildly: 'What are you going to do now?'

'Get behind them. They can shoot through our bows till they run out of shooting. It will mess up the cabin but come nowhere near sinking her. Nor will it reach us here.' She tapped the bulkhead. 'Whoever built this boat built her well.'

The other had begun to move forward for the Belgian had been thinking less quickly. Molina said:

'You're the captain, dear.'

'Then be good enough to turn the spare tank on.' She had noticed that he hadn't done so. 'And Charles, you keep your head down sensibly.'

Russell was out of his depth but enjoying it. It pleased him to be given orders provided the giver knew his business. As Helen very clearly did. 'But suppose they won't play that game?'

'They'll have to. We're a good deal faster—they can't break away.' She stood up as they came astern of the other but keeping her head below the bulkhead, looking out in quick sightings, as cool as a surgeon. Two bullets thumped into the galley forward. 'Much good may that do them.' She looked down at the two sprawling men. 'Gentlemen, you may now get up. But keep on either side of me here. Here where it's safe behind fine thick mahogany even if they hole us forward.'

The other boat had swung to port. Helen Monteath swung to port behind her.

Charles Russell nodded. 'I think I get it. Like one of those RAF films after the war. The Spitfire gets behind the Heinkel but it can't get its guns to bear on the turn. So round and round they go like crazy——'

'Something like that. Except we've no guns.' She might have added 'Thanks to you', but she was a tactful and generous-spirited woman.

'But we can't go round and round for ever.'

'I haven't the least intention of doing so. One of two things is going to happen. Either they break away or they don't. If they break away that suits us fine. We've got what we came to get—confirmation. Everything happens as Molina said it did. There's no point in hanging about conspicuously and perhaps getting chased by that launch and those gendarmes.'

'Agreed,' Russell said. 'But if they don't break?'

'Then I'm going to make a feint to ram them.'

'Suppose they don't buy it?'

'They'll have to buy it.' She spoke in a tone of total confidence. 'We're faster than they are, more solidly built, and it's a very long swim indeed to the shore. All terrorists are the same in practice. They take hostages and sometimes kill them; they bomb aircraft and murder innocent people; and they boast their own lives are of no account. But they *are* of account when it comes to the crunch. Can you think of more than a handful of cases where terrorists have shot it right out? I learnt that from an Israeli boy friend and it's the basis of his country's policy.'

'You sound very sure of it.'

'Yes I am.'

'It's Molina's boat.'

He laughed. 'Please accept it.'

The turns had begun to tighten increasingly. 'They've the better rudder,' Helen said. 'We're the faster but they've the smaller turn. If we sideslip we'll be sitting ducks and in any case there's a limit to this.' She made her mind up in an instant decision. 'I'm going in to ram,' she said.

For the first time she opened the throttle fully and the interval between them shrank. Russell was helping to hold the wheel down.

They were down to five yards when two more shots came. The Japanese had learnt his lesson. Now he was shooting high for the windshield. He smashed it but it was above their heads. A splinter cut Helen's arm. She didn't flinch.

'Would you like me to take her?'

'No. Keep your head down.'

Twelve feet, ten feet, six feet. A final shot. Suddenly the Belgian straightened.

Instantly there were yards between them, the angle a full ninety degrees. Helen hadn't eased the throttle and the gap was increasing as Russell watched it. The cockpit was exposed again but Russell said happily: 'Well out of pistol range. If they'd anything bigger than that they'd have used it.'

He took the wheel from Helen Monteath and Molina bound up her forearm neatly. It was evident that the wound wasn't serious. 'That'll hold till ten o'clock this morning when the doctor's coming up to see Campbell. But I don't think you're going to need any stitching.'

He spoke in a solicitous murmur but Russell had excellent hearing and caught it. 'Campbell,' Molina was saying, 'James Campbell. We'll have more than one question to ask of Campbell.'

10

By the time Charles Russell reached the Bleiner the feeling of dawn was mysteriously stirring. He did not feel inclined for sleep but the night porter made him coffee and sandwiches. Over them he considered unhappily.

Unhappily because he was near to failure. He had come to this depressing town to reassure his friend the General that what looked like a plan to destroy the West was in fact no more than that plan's appearance. Not that the ghost would be impotent. No. If it couldn't be shown to be a ghost there were men who would act as though it were real, and Charles Russell who knew their country's history was a long way from dismissing them as men who were foolishly over-insuring. So he had to establish that something *wasn't*, always a difficult thing to do, and moreover he was a long way from doing it.

On the contrary events had moved against him. Lenterheims was German controlled and Lenterheims was recycling plutonium. That plutonium came across the lake and at one point was alarmingly vulnerable. Men who would shoot at intruders had gathered, they'd gone out on the lake to make a reconnaissance, and behind them they'd left an armoury which suggested much more than casual violence. The mere presence of such men was frightening though no doubt that could be argued both ways. If you accepted the Colonel-General's hypothesis (Russell found himself thinking of 'hope' not 'hypothesis') they could still be a part of the cast of a play, a necessary part at that, but if the play were real life they'd be necessary to real-life action. And behind them there was always that armoury.

Should he signal all this to the General? He decided against it. His business was to assess a position, not to report to a formal superior the daily events which he'd be hearing from Helen. Moreover they must see Campbell again and after that, if he had to, he'd reconsider. At the worst he could always bow out.

But he wouldn't.

They saw Campbell at ten o'clock that morning. James Campbell was looking a good deal stronger and Russell told him what had happened shortly. When he had finished James Campbell smiled wryly.

'It looks as though I'd been talking some nonsense. You remember what I said in London about the possibilities of a nuclear hijack?' He had a formidable memory and began to quote himself. ' "I can't deny it's on in theory—any hijacking is on in theory—but I don't believe it's on in practice. All countries are aware of the risks. And plutonium is radioactive, so to steal it from a nuclear power station would need a body of skilled and protected scientists who would also need to be highly trained infantrymen. The combination is somewhat uncommon." ' He smiled against himself again. 'That's beginning to look decidedly shaky.'

'But granted that these men have arms, even granted that they have skill in the use of them, I would doubt if they are also scientists.'

'But they're not stealing from a nuclear power station,

the plutonium has already left it. It will be insulated and therefore handleable.'

'In containers?' Russell asked.

'Indeed. As it happens one of the very best insulators is an ordinary sheet of unglazed paper, but that's more than a little academic since sheets of paper are hardly robust. They use something more sophisticated and that something goes into a strong outer casing. Very strong indeed, I assure you. It's subjected to a fifty foot fall, then put into a swimming bath, dropped on a spike and put in a fire. Now that,' James Campbell concluded dourly, 'is really quite a strong container.'

'Strong enough for non-scientists to steal it without committing suicide?'

'But I wouldn't care to store it privately. Or not for an indefinite time.'

'A scientist could still use it later?'

'Certainly, but hardly secretly. He'd need a laboratory, even a plant.'

Charles Russell fell into deep reflection and Helen slipped away to make coffee. Molina was smoking in silence, fascinated. He had a taste for adventure and this was a high one. It was also, by his standards, bizarre. He had a hard time not showing disbelief but he was courteous and his face showed nothing.

When Helen returned Charles Russell asked Campbell: 'So where do you think they're going to take it?'

'Geographically they've two choices—here or Germany. But Switzerland is out of the question. The Swiss would have to be in with the hijacking and I imagine you find that as wild as I do. So that leaves us with Germany—back to Germany.'

'Where it couldn't be handled in secret?'

'No.'

'But it might be with official connivance?'

'Ye-es,' Campbell said but he sounded doubtful.

Charles Russell too had a very fair memory. 'I refute that out of your own wise mouth.' He too began to quote and accurately. 'I said once "If Germany tried to make the Bomb——" and your answer was, "She is much too sensible."'

'Then some crazy neo-Nazi group?'

'With laboratories, scientists, all the trimmings?'

James Campbell shook his head; he was tiring. 'It doesn't begin to make ordinary sense.'

Helen had seen the first signs of exhaustion and rose at once. The two men followed her. They thanked James Campbell politely and went downstairs. Molina was the first to speak.

'Campbell was right. It doesn't make sense.'

'It makes sense if we assume the worst which is that somebody's trying to make a weapon, and the evidence doesn't exclude just that. But I'm not prepared to accept it yet. Therefore there's a piece still missing and therefore we have got to find it. I wish we knew more of what Lenterheims does.'

'It seems agreed that they recycle plutonium.'

'Probably they do. But how much?'

Helen Monteath said. 'I'll go and ask Campbell. If I slip up alone it shouldn't disturb him.'

'If I'd thought he would know I'd have asked him myself.' Charles Russell, for once, was a little brusque. 'He hasn't himself been over Lenterheims and even if he knew their capacity he wouldn't know how much is fed into it. Twice weekly according to what we know.

Containers in a special vehicle. But how many containers? *How much plutonium?*'

In the silence which followed Molina rose. He was sensitive and therefore tactful and he guessed that the other two wished to talk privately. Molina took no exception to that. He knew that Helen Monteath was an agent, and though he hadn't put it in terms he had given her, by implication, his blessing to complete her mission. Charles Russell was clearly her boss and he liked him. Molina was with them now but not one of them. He had made a shrewd guess at what was happening, though not as it happened a quite complete one, and it was natural they couldn't tell him everything. Why should they? He wasn't one of their trade.

So he rose and smiled pleasantly. 'You know where to find me.'

When he had gone Charles Russell said: 'That's a very nice man you've found yourself here.'

'Here? I don't like the sound of that at all.'

'Then a very nice man in any place.'

'That's better—that's more like Charles Russell. Indeed he's a very nice man, dear Charles, and in more ways than you're likely to know.'

'Congratulations, then.'

'A little early. But that wasn't what you wanted to talk about.' She gave him a hard but friendly stare. 'Charles, you've got one of your famous hunches.'

'Not a hunch exactly—just a feeling of absence. A piece which isn't there. We must find it.'

'We?'

'But of course. Are you free tomorrow?'

'All but tomorrow night.'

'I meant the night.'

'When another load comes over?'

'Precisely.'

She thought it over, smiling secretly. 'Molina will be disappointed.'

'You can compensate Molina amply.'

'I'm under your orders,' she said.

'This isn't one.'

'That makes it all the more of an order.'

In the event they left Neuwald on Wednesday evening, not taking the ferry across the lake but motoring round the northern road. Helen had been driving sedately for Russell disliked high speeds at any time and on foreign roads he loathed them actively. They went through the German frontier normally and later turned sharply back beyond the lake. They were running along its opposite shore and Russell had brought a large scale map. He was reading this and watching the signposts.

'We need to cut roughly north-east, I think. That should bring us out on the main road to Ulm but I'd like to strike it well below that. If the contours are right it's rolling country, or rolling enough to find some fold where we can hide but also watch the main road.'

They saw it almost at once: it was perfect. Too perfect as they were later to find, a choice which another man would spot quickly, a slope overlooking a bend in the road, an unobscured view over stony fields with a deserted smallholder's cottage capping the rise.

They drove up a track and concealed the car in a barn which had long since lost its roof. Charles Russell went over the cottage carefully, using his torch when obliged to do so. It had crumbled, deserted for generations, but in the courtyard there was still a well. The wellhead tackle had fallen in ruin but it hadn't been sealed and Charles Russell looked down it. At the bottom was brackish and hostile water and Russell dropped a stone in curiously. From the echo the water was still quite deep.

They went back to the slope and chose their lookout, the cottage fifteen yards behind them. On the journey Charles Russell had spoken little and Helen had respected his silence, but now as the moon came up she asked: 'It's the convoy we've come to see?'

He nodded. He was thinking what he had said before, that in this matter there could be high security but hardly any degree of secrecy. There couldn't be, you couldn't conceal them, not armoured cars and armed men in lorries. You could move them by night and that was all, but even by night you couldn't hide what Charles Russell had come here to see.

He corrected himself. You couldn't hide what he *hoped* to see. Not from a man who had once been a soldier.

'You're being very mysterious, Charles.'

'Perhaps, but I promise it isn't a tease. I need a second opinion, you see, and if I tell you what I suspect you'll look for it. That isn't what I want at all. I want somebody seeing with innocent eyes.'

. . . As my late enemy and friend the General sent me to Neuwald to form an opinion. He told me nothing to prejudice honest judgement.

They settled to wait and soon they heard it, the distant rumble of heavy and closely spaced vehicles. The curve of the road was against their seeing them but they could see the glow of unhooded lights. The convoy was driving with headlights, openly, and Russell allowed a quick nod of relief. The last vehicle would light the next and so on up the grinding convoy. For it wasn't travelling fast—that too was good. The more detail they could see the better.

Lying beside him Helen frowned. Some instinct had inexplicably stirred, the instinct which told a feral animal of some danger neither seen nor smelt, or perhaps it was meticulous training. For this wasn't quite right, it really wasn't—not lying together like this, uncovered. She was sure enough they hadn't been followed for Russell would have spotted that too, but this flew in the face of all her training quite apart from her increasing unease. She said to Charles Russell: 'Excuse me, please. I'm going up to the farm a moment.'

He misunderstood her: she had meant him to do so.

The convoy was coming round the bend, the first vehicle clear in the lights of the second. It was a Jeep with a heavy machine-gun mounted ahead. The gunner traversed the barrel ritually and his Number Two was holding the belt. The vehicle behind, Russell thought, would by all the rules be an armoured car. Then a lorry carrying infantry, then the vehicle which really mattered. More troops in a second lorry. Another Jeep.

And that would conclude the entertainment if that was what it really was.

Helen slipped quietly back to the cottage. She had noticed a loft with a window, a ladder. The floorboards would be rotten as matchwood but a joist or two might still bear her weight. In any case she must make that window for the voice of her instinct was now a scream.

And she had disobeyed Russell's explicit orders. She

hadn't liked it in the cabin cruiser; she hadn't enjoyed being shot at helplessly.

She reached the window and crouched behind the sill. She hadn't brought her handsome handbag—Charles Russell would have noticed that—but she had another place to put the pistol.

The Japanese had hidden cleverly. She didn't see him till he began his rush.

Several hundred miles north the German major had been checking the convoy with a sort of bored thoroughness. He but not his two subaltern officers, certainly not the troops they commanded, had the knowledge which was causing his boredom. For he thought that this drill was overdone, too often to have continuing value. Not that he resented drill, for as a Prussian it was as deep in his blood as service to the German state. But this convoy wasn't proper soldiering and his family had been *Totenkopf* since the mind of good Prussians ran not to the contrary. He had no contacts with the new aristocracy, the rich salesmen and even richer merchants who now held the power his own caste had once owned. Such a background was dead in the Federal Republic, a millstone rather than what it once had been, and the major suspected it had cost him promotion. Nevertheless he checked meticulously since he wasn't the kind to skimp a duty. Then he climbed into the armoured car, opening the hatch and standing. He waved to the convoy to move and it started.

He was bored and the Japanese had been more so. He had some English but the two Spaniards had none, and as for the Belgian he didn't get on with him, despising him for the ex-bourgeois he was. He loathed playing cards and waiting idly, so as Belami Clark had thought he would he had found himself something to do to keep interested. He didn't share Charles Russell's hunch that something was very wrong with the convoy; he *knew* that it wasn't what it seemed. Clark's informant had sold him the knowledge dearly, but he'd sold it and Clark had passed it on to the only other man he trusted. So this strange convoy came down the road from Ulm and the Japanese had decided to have a look at it. It could do no harm and would keep him occupied.

He went over by the last of the ferries, intending to return next morning. It would be pleasant to get away from those Spaniards, that Belgian whom he'd never liked, and the thought of a night in the open appealed to him.

The site which Charles Russell had chosen was excellent. Too excellent—the Japanese found it too. He had arrived before Charles Russell and Helen and at first he hadn't troubled to hide since he wasn't expecting others to join him. But when he noticed a car climb up to the smallholding he slipped into a hollow and waited. A man and a woman came out of it quietly. The man used his torch from time to time, but always on the ground, with discretion, and the moon was never strong enough for recognizing people's faces at a matter of maybe a hundred yards. But the Japanese was by nature suspicious. There'd been two men and a woman out on the lake. True there was only one man now, but why were this man and woman here at all? Poking about in deserted smallholdings, apparently settling down to watch. And what was this couple intending to watch? It could only be what he'd come for himself and in that case they could only be enemies.

He wasn't armed but that didn't trouble him. He knew how to kill with his hands if he had to.

Charles Russell was watching the convoy through nightglasses. There was a moon but in fact it was barely helpful for the convoy still had its headlights on, each vehicle clear in the glare of the next one. To his surprise it halted directly in front of him, the leading Jeep stopping without a signal. He considered this halt and finally nodded. This was what he would have done himself if this convoy were really what he suspected. If it wasn't he wouldn't have bothered with checkpoints; he'd have driven as fast as he dared for the ferry.

What happened next confirmed this strongly. The major climbed out of the armoured car, took a quick salute from the leading Jeep, then turned the infantry out of the escort lorries which sandwiched the essential vehicle. Their subalterns formed them up: they presented arms. Very smart, Russell thought, but surely unnecessary. Then the major and the two junior officers walked up to what looked like a prison van. There was meshing to shield the two drivers who didn't get out. Charles Russell, who couldn't hear it, guessed.

'Do you recognize?'

'I recognize, Herr Major.'

'Do you recognize these officers?'

'Sir.'

'But we will give you the password.'

Evidently they gave it correctly ('God knows what would happen if somebody flunked it. In anything not quite out of the book German infantry is inclined to flap'). The three officers walked to the rear of the van.

Where there was more and too parade-ground saluting. The major produced a key on a chain and one of the subalterns solemnly signed for it. Then he opened the van and went inside. He came out in perhaps a couple of minutes; he stood at attention and waited orders, and again Charles Russell could hear them mentally.

'All present and correct?'

'Herr Major.'

'Then you may seal again and embus your men.'

. . . All present and correct? Well, all present. There could hardly be any doubt of that but 'correct' depended on what you meant by it. Just training and drill or a real live run with the deadly stuff that really mattered.

Russell had reached his conclusion from what he'd seen; he looked round for Helen Monteath. She had not come back and Charles Russell frowned. He knew that women took longer than men but she must have been away five minutes and it was a pity she had missed the charade. He would have valued an independent opinion, indeed that was why he had brought her here, and the convoy had begun to move again.

As it did so the Japanese started his rush. In the lights of the convoy he'd recognized Russell. He had seen him only once, on the lake, but that once had been enough for certainty. To a simple mind it was very simple. Russell was an enemy. Kill.

He hadn't seen Helen slip back to the cottage, but he had taken off his shoes and socks and Russell didn't hear him coming till he was almost on him, retreat impossible. He half rose to his feet but a blow sent him spinning. He fell on his face and the Japanese pinned him.

That Russell survived was a fortunate accident. The Japanese could have broken his neck at once but he didn't intend an easy death. Charles Russell felt fingers feeling expertly, then a sudden and physically blinding pain. He cried out in agony; somebody laughed. He didn't hear Helen's first shot which missed. But the Japanese did and he paid no attention. He was more than a little berserk by now, the lust to make an enemy suffer much stronger than any instinct to save himself. Charles Russell felt his fingers again. The same shattering pain and this time he fainted.

He came to with his head in Helen's lap. The other was lying beside them, motionless. Helen asked softly: 'Your neck?'

He felt it. 'He doesn't seem to have broken it but I'm going to be stiff for quite a while.'

'I'll take you to Molina's doctor.'

Normally he'd have protested; now he didn't. He was still in some pain and dizzy, not focusing. He could hear that it was Helen Monteath but see only a woman's uncertain outline. Who said anxiously: 'Can you walk?'

'I can try.' He tried to move his legs. They obeyed him. It was doubtful if they would carry him yet but perhaps after five or ten minutes' rest . . . .

He looked at the Japanese beside them. 'Quite dead?' he inquired. His voice was steadying.

'Oh yes, he's very dead indeed.'

She leant down and went over the body carefully, removing its papers, its ring and its dentures. Then she threw it across her shoulder casually. He was a smallish man and she a big woman. 'That well,' she explained, 'the one at the farm. It's very unprofessional, but nobody seems to come here often and if he's what we think he is none of his friends will dare to come after him. In two or three months. . . .'

She left it at that.

She was back in ten minutes. 'You're feeling better?'

'Better enough to thank you sincerely.'

'Actually I owe an apology. I'm sorry I missed the first time. That was bad.'

'The light was lousy,' Charles Russell said.

11

Next morning Charles Russell's neck was in plaster but his mind was working a vigorous overtime. Helen sat by his bedside and listened demurely.

'A great pity you didn't see all the show.'

'I saw a little when I wasn't covering you.'

'I repeat I'm extremely grateful you did. But what did you think of what you saw?'

'I thought it was bogus,' Helen said.

The word appeared to surprise Charles Russell but he recovered and waved a hand to go on. 'Elucidate,' he said.

'If I can. I thought it was a bit like Aldershot—all the Brass in a stand with a band in front of them, the banging about and shouting orders. Nothing serious was really happening.'

'You're very observant indeed. Go on.'

'I've nothing else to go on about.'

'No conclusion from your impression?'

'No. Conclusions,' Helen Monteath added firmly, 'are a matter I'd rather leave to you.'

He sat up in bed though he wasn't supposed to. 'The charade last night was a dummy run.'

'I don't think I get it.'

'It's perfectly simple. They were carrying something or even nothing, but whatever they had it wasn't plutonium.'

She thought it over, frowning and puzzled. 'But that makes a total nonsense of everything.'

'But does it? Let's start from the beginning of everything. Clark's basic plan is one of *embroilment*, to force your master's hawks to act from fear. I needn't enlarge on fear of what, which is that somebody German is making the Bomb.'

'James Campbell thought that was out politically.'

'I know he did and so do I.'

She spread her hands. 'You're talking in riddles.'

'I'm trying to lead you along the path of reason. If you catch me in a *non sequitur* stop me.'

'I'll do just that,' she said.

'Very well. So the plan of embroilment is based on suspicion and that has been built up efficiently. First they snatch a nuclear scientist and bring him to Neuwald where Lenterheims operates. Lenterheims is German controlled and plutonium is being recycled there. A consignment is hijacked——'

'I thought you said——'

'Oh no, I didn't—not at all. I accept that plutonium goes in to Lenterheims but I don't accept that every convoy is carrying the real thing in that van. How much plutonium Lenterheims handles is something James Campbell couldn't tell us and in any case it's not a factor. Or it isn't if you concede the premise that some of those convoys are dummy runs.'

She thought it over and finally nodded. 'To the German military mind——'

'Just so. They've a considerable army and soldiers need exercise. Even so small a thing as a convoy takes a company out of its barracks at night.'

'But I think I *have* caught you out,' Helen said.

159

'That's why I'm dragging you through this hoop.'

'If some of the convoys are really dummies Clark and his men may not know which are real ones.'

'Not if they have information. To know what's going on at all Clark must have an informant in Germany, and if he knows enough to tell him the dates he will know enough to pick him a good one.'

'A night the real thing is coming over?'

'No, not at all. They'll pick a dummy. What they're after is a load of rubbish.'

Helen Monteath had stood up in protest. Her voice was one of flat incredulity. 'But Charles——'

'Please sit down again and let me finish. To make James Campbell's other point, what would Clark do with real live plutonium?'

'What would he do with a can of bricks?'

'Nothing. But it's a great deal less dicey. And who's to say that it's not the real thing?'

'The Germans——'

'Precisely. You have it precisely.' Russell slapped the sheet with an open hand. *'And what Russian is going to believe their denial?* Consider it against the whole background—Campbell being snatched, then Lenterheims. Which is German controlled and does recycle. A consignment is hijacked and disappears and the hot lines start to melt from the traffic. And what is the German story? Preposterous. Or preposterous against that background.' He began to mimic a German voice, one minute arrogant, the next almost cringing. 'Yes, I admit we were sending the stuff to Lenterheims but we had nothing whatever to do with the hijack. Further, it wasn't really a hijack. On that particular night we were running old catsmeat.' He resumed his normal voice but forcefully. 'You work for the General, you know their minds. So if you were a Russian would you believe that?'

'No,' Helen said with decision. 'Certainly not.' She considered before she spoke again. 'It's really a very slick plan indeed.'

'Clark has had plenty of time to mature it.'

'So what do we do now?'

'I don't know.'

It was a rare thing for Russell to say but he meant it. He felt frustrated but he was also amused, for the irony appealed to his humour. He'd been sent here to reassure the General, but reassurance was now out of the question whichever way Clark had chosen to play it. If he'd chosen to hijack real plutonium Charles Russell would have had to report it, the plain opposite of reassurance; and now that he was going to fake it the General's colleagues wouldn't believe the faking. Charles Russell laughed but it wasn't a happy one.

Helen Monteath had been thinking too. 'How do you think Clark means to do it?'

'I can only say what I'd do myself, given the arms which we know they possess. I'd slip out at night and rocket the ferry just after the German guard had been changed. Not to sink her with all hands at once since that would sink their objective too but enough to cause a total panic in the crew and the not very high class Swiss escort. Then I'd force my way on board in the rumpus, blow the lock of that van and take what I wanted. That presupposes a man who could do it but they'd hardly overlook the point. At a guess I would rather fancy that Dutchman.'

'And then?' Helen asked.

'Then anyone still alive on the ferry will be left to fend for himself as he can. Clark will take his container and probably dump it since it isn't, in itself, of use. Then he'll make for the German side at once.'

'The changed German guard will be doing the same. They'll have heard the shooting so won't they go after him?'

'That's a risk but Belami Clark will have thought of it. The timing will have to be pretty accurate to let the soldiers get out of effective chasing range, but Clark knows their course to the German side—straight back to the point of embarkation—so he's sure to steer away at an angle. And in any case, as we know ourselves, there's often fog on the lake at this time of the year. No, I'd say he'd a very fair chance of slipping them.'

'And when he gets to the German side, what then?'

'They beach the boat and disperse as arranged. The boat will be identified quickly and a canister has gone from the ferry . . . .' Charles Russell shrugged. 'The balloon rises vertically.'

Helen Monteath said: 'We've got to stop it.'

'Of course we have but consider the snags. If we go to the Swiss we both know what will happen. They could deal with those men hiding up in that house, especially if they catch them with arms, but they're only the supporting cast and for that I've a certain crazy sympathy. Clark is the man who really matters: if they don't get Clark he can try again. But what have they got on Clark? Just nothing. Or nothing unless we tell them things which would inevitably involve Molina. What's been happening at his house, for instance—James Campbell and how we got him away. And that lets Molina down unfairly since I doubt if the Swiss would let him stay here. He wouldn't like that and nor would you.'

She thought it over and nodded reluctantly. 'I wish I could think of something else.'

He said with an unusual harshness, the aftermath of a good deal of pain: 'You don't have to think. You just report.'

'Meaning by that?'

'I beg your pardon. But you've been signalling to the General daily?'

'Naturally. He knows the score.'

'Have you told him about the dummy runs?'

'We only worked that out this morning.'

'Then go down to the Bleiner, please, and signal again. Make it Most Immediate and leave your General to make the decisions.'

When this message arrived on the General's desk he re-read it with an increasing alarm. He saw at once what Russell had seen, that this development turned everything inside out. What he'd hoped for was confirmation from Russell that a bluff was being put up which he could call; or if he couldn't call it outright he had hoped to convince his nervous hawks that it was something which could be safely ignored. But he couldn't do that now, he'd been trapped. . . . Tell them there was a plan to hijack, a plan in a high degree of readiness, but as it happened it wouldn't be real plutonium, just a dummy run and a load of nothing. . . .

He wouldn't last long after that, he really wouldn't.

Like Russell he had a disciplined mind so he put that behind him and started again. Time was in one sense on his side, for according to Helen the next run was on

Tuesday. That gave him adequate room to make his arrangements but in another sense time was running against him. He'd been given ten days and these weren't yet up, but he had very good sources of information and he knew that troops had already been moving. Not into action yet—into readiness. In the world which he lived in that didn't surprise him, but he was still an important and useful official and on the whole he was inclined to doubt if anyone would give final orders before his ten days had run out and destroyed him.

Which was also, he remembered, on Tuesday.

So this was a new situation; he'd meet it. They were putting him to the Question, were they? Well, he couldn't defeat the machine, he wouldn't try. But at least he could destroy his tormentors, this Clark and the men he had hired to help him. In the new circumstances there was no other course.

He began to consider the method coolly. He needn't tell his colleagues anything—no soldiers dropped by parachute, later snatched back again. His own people could go by commercial airline. Of course they would have to speak German fluently and they would also have convincing Swiss passports. If one of them died he'd be stripped and left, and if wounded, well, he would know the rules. The others would hide and come out at leisure. All would be highly trained and competent.

The question, then, was of organization. The General must make perfectly sure.

He picked up a telephone.

Belami Clark was reflecting too, for although in a very different way events had moved against him also. He didn't know the worst of them, that Molina had cased the house and its armoury, but he knew enough to be deeply disturbing.

To begin with he'd lost the Japanese. He'd gone out one night and he hadn't returned and that was all the others could tell him, but to Belami Clark the grim deduction was as clear as though he had had it on paper. Russell or maybe Molina's woman had picked up his lieutenant and killed him. Which meant that they were far from negligible. Once he'd thought they could do little. Not now.

Clark sighed for the blow was by no means a small one. His commitment did not allow affection but in so far as he could feel attachment that attachment was to the Japanese. It would be impossible to replace him now, for the two men still to come from Germany had never been in his class or near it.

And the second unwelcome complication was that affray on the lake which he hadn't ordered. It had been foolish to indulge in gunplay—the Japanese had a weakness for shooting first—but before he'd been murdered the Japanese (Clark thought of 'murder' without hypocrisy) had passed to Belami Clark by radio an account of that night's unfortunate outcome and a description of a man and a woman who were almost certainly Russell and Helen. So the third in that boat must have been Molina and an hour or two before he'd been fishing. He could have picked up the others to take them out peacefully. . . .

No, that was too easy, too much to hope for. It was much safer to assume the worst, that they'd gone out to make some kind of reconnaissance. Then they'd have seen the ferry and how the guard changed and they'd had very good reason to see his own men. They could hardly have guessed his plan in detail, not without finding his secret armoury, but they'd have seen enough to add two and two and Charles Russell would certainly make them four. And four spelt a hijack in any language.

It was a serious setback, he mustn't blind himself, and for a moment he considered postponement. Call it all off for the moment and wait ? But wait for what—another chance? He'd no reason to think it would ever come, and even if perhaps it did it would be very unlikely to be like this one where the pieces had meshed together so neatly, so convincingly to support a deception.

So the risks had increased and increased uncomfortably but he'd gone too far to draw back now even if he'd had time to do so. And he hadn't so very much longer to live. A doctor had recently told him that. He'd believed him since the pain had grown worse. Moreover he was losing weight fast.

He began to consider the third of his difficulties. It was in no way his fault; it was one of manpower. The four in the hideout were now down to three, which made five when he added himself and the Dutchman. Five men were not enough; seven might be.

And he could only make seven if the other two came to him, the two who had still to arrive from Germany. One was a Japanese again though nowhere near the dead one's class, the other the third unreliable Spaniard.

Belami Clark didn't often swear but now he permitted a blasphemous blast. For he *had* called them up, he had even sent money, and when they hadn't arrived he'd protested peremptorily. And what had they answered? Clark swore again savagely. They had said that they'd never received the money. Clark was certain they had and of what they had done with it. They had lost it playing poker out of their class.

It was idle to blame compulsive gamblers so he'd have to send them some more and he didn't have it. Buying the boat had drained him dry and he had barely enough for the other three's food.

He almost smiled—that would not be so difficult. It would be fruitless to ask Molina for more but he didn't intend to ask Molina; he intended to take from Molina while he could. After all he was still in his house. It was easy.

As it happened Charles Russell had guessed correctly. It was the Dutchman who was at home with explosives.

12

Charles Russell's neck was out of plaster so the discomfort he felt was in no way physical. But mentally he wasn't at ease. His conscience was clear, he'd done the only thing possible, which was to tell the Colonel-General everything and leave the next move to him. Quite so. But unhappily Russell could guess that move, and something quite close to regret nagged remorselessly.

For he'd meant it when he'd told Helen Monteath that he'd a certain crazy sympathy for the desperate men whom Clark had collected. Urban guerrillas? He snorted. No such thing. Urban guerrillas had money behind them, clear objectives and an organization. Russell held them in a very real horror, though less for their mostly cowardly crimes than for their smugness and intolerable double-talk. They prated of lost lands. No doubt. But how had these lands in fact been lost? Had another state attacked them ruthlessly? On the contrary that state had been four times assaulted. What Russell would not accept was the humbug, the pose of a sort of latterday Poland dismembered by imperialist Powers.

But these men of Clark's weren't guerrillas of any kind. Come to think of it they were nothing at all, the flotsam of a formless philosophy which would pull down the pillars and dance in the rubble. Russell would have agreed with Clark. They were the necessary hired hands of violence, but at least they weren't shams and one shouldn't despise them.

Russell frowned and stirred in his chair unhappily. For he knew what was going to happen and hated it. It was odd what retirement did to a man. In his service he'd sent men to their deaths and it hadn't disturbed a well disciplined conscience, but in this case he had given no orders; he had merely connived and that was unworthy. Not that there weren't excuses: there always were. He had accepted a limited task and failed in it, and he wasn't in any sense the General's man. Who wouldn't have listened if he'd offered advice in circumstances which had changed completely, and indeed he had no advice to offer. The General could now do only one thing and Russell didn't doubt that he'd do it.

He began to consider the probable method. . . . Send men into that house and shoot it out? But no, that would be a little crude. Not that the General would shrink from crudity but he'd try to avoid any complications. Which there always were after any gunfight—bodies there mightn't be time to dispose of, the certainty of police inquiries plus the likelihood of a row in the Press. For which the General cared nothing whatever but which annoyed him when it got it wrong as in this case it was bound to do. The Press couldn't be told the truth. It would never print it.

Besides, there was always Clark, the real danger. He never went to the deserted house, so except by coincidence he wouldn't be there; and the Colonel-General was too experienced to play coincidences in a matter like this. He'd wait till they were all together. . . .

Tuesday morning in the small hours—the hijack.

Russell saw it with a sickening clarity, Clark's boat with five men if he took the Dutchman, another stolen boat standing off in the mist. The frogmen slipping overboard, timing it, submerging till Clark's cruiser was near them. The masked faces coming out of the water like some mythical animal man had forgotten, then the volley of grenades to the cockpit. Some would be fragmentation, some incendiary. The cries of the wounded, the roar as the tank went. Men struggling in a blazing pool, away for a moment, then caught again helplessly.

An accident of course, just an accident. Nothing to prove it was other than that. The stolen boat back at its usual moorings, all traces of the frogmen gone. Nobody alive to tell of them. Perhaps wounds on any bodies still floating, but what would the police make of that? They'd make nothing. They might make guesses and construct a theory; they might even tell their masters what it was.

And their masters would turn their heads away. It was an accident, wasn't it? Leave it at that. Bury what's left for we don't want a scandal. Not here in this right little, tight little Switzerland.

Russell was familiar with violence. It wasn't men's deaths which offended him; he'd seen plenty of those and they'd left him unshaken. What nagged at him now was a sense of propriety. Moderation was very important indeed and he himself would have acted differently. He'd have gone for Clark, let the others go. Cut off the head and the body was helpless. Clark had the brains, the real malice, the drive. The others were no more than small fry. They'd go back to their squalid killings and kidnappings, go on scratching a surface they couldn't dent.

Deplorable, no doubt. Quite wrong. Charles Russell mistrusted all moral judgements, but the world had to pay for its evident evils.

But not an outrageous price. Not Clark.

Two men sat again in the oval room but this time the second wasn't the chunky man. He was much better known though in fact not more powerful and an anxious world followed his travels with scepticism. He was evidently not an Old American but he always put America first. Even his bitter and numerous enemies would concede that he put his own country first.

And that was just all they'd concede to the second man.

The first behind the desk said: 'Well?'

The other didn't like his manner, it was altogether too sharp and determined. In a matter of ten days or so he'd changed from a hesitant fumbling uncertainty to a brisk and almost offensive decision. But that was all too simply explicable. He'd won at his Convention hands down and the polls showed him running three lengths ahead. He was going to get in again—that was near certain. He knew it and wasn't standing for double talk.

'They've been moving troops,' the new man said.

'Berlin, I suppose.'

'No, not Berlin, it's much more serious.' He began to explain since he loved his own voice, 'Berlin is a sort of standing stake—they leave it on the table, frozen. Like the evens after a roulette zero . . . . Go into Cuba, we'll pinch out Berlin. It served them then and will serve them again.'

'I asked you where they were moving troops.'

'All over. On a very broad front.'

The man behind the desk banged it hard. ' "Broad front"—that means nothing. It's jargon and you're not a soldier.'

'There's much more than is usual the wrong side of Berlin and increasing concentrations west of Prague.'

'That's happened before and nothing came of it.'

'This time they may mean business.'

'Why?'

'I think you know that already.'

'Maybe I do. But I'd like to hear how you put it yourself.'

'According to all our information they're suspicious that Germany's making the Bomb.'

'And do you believe she is?'

'I doubt it. She is sensibly governed and has too much to lose. But it comes to the same thing, you see, if the suspicion is sufficiently strong.'

'Or even,' the man at the desk said grimly, 'or even if our friends want excuses.'

'That strikes me as a trifle cynical. Our friends, as you call them, have suffered grievously. I wouldn't find it in my heart to blame them——'

'Do you have children?'

'You know I have children.'

'Then I suggest that you start to think of them. Now. Stop listening to your wet diplomats. Talk sense.'

The other relapsed into sulky silence. He'd never much liked the man at the desk, he had always been distressingly corny, and this new manner of his was hard to take for an official with delicate egghead nerves. But there was nothing he could do about that. Without his job he'd be lost and he meant to keep it. After the silence he asked politely: 'You've seen the Top Brass?'

'Of course I have. And they told me what I already knew. If there's any sort of attack in strength we can only stop it by firing the Tacticals.'

'When they'll fire the bigger ones.'

'Yes, they will. But not, or not at first, at us.'

'At our allies?'

'We have only one. That's Germany which will take the hard knocks. The rest will run like rats, France first.'

'There's always diplomacy.'

'No there is not—not if you're right and this is serious.' The man at the desk was losing his temper. 'All you fancypants have the same delusion. You believe your job is somehow different, a sort of independent power. And it isn't, you just oil the works. When those gum up it depends on the soldiers.'

The second man sighed, he had heard this before. Privately he couldn't deny it but it offended him hearing it put so brutally. He asked wearily: 'Then what will you do?'

'One of the coloured Alerts. And we'll leak it.'

'That's bluff, I'm afraid.'

'Have you never played poker?'

'Last time we did it the world attacked us.'

'Rubbish, the world did no such thing. We were savaged by the left wing Press. How many divisions do *they* have? Tell me.'

'World opinion——' the new man said stiffly.

'Crap.'

'And what'll you do if they call your hand?'

'I don't know now but I'll certainly pray. If I'm forced to I'll press the buttons. All of them.'

'Jesus in heaven.'

'Yes. Jesus in heaven. Jesus and Mary and all the saints.' He looked across his desk with fierce contempt. 'You rootless men know nothing whatever. You don't feel things in your guts—you don't have them. You call on the Almighty freely but you haven't a single claim on his mercy.'

'You'd do that alone?'

'I'd have to do it.' The manner changed with a startling suddenness from furious anger to near-urbanity. 'That's one of the less agreeable penalties for pretending to be an open society.'

Molina had much in common with Russell, including a firm belief in thinking asleep. He liked to marshal his problem and look at it squarely, then he'd go to bed and sleep like a child. It was astonishing how often next morning the solution would be as clear as the dawn. But he had to sleep alone to do it: distractions however pleasant destroyed the magic. So tonight he had made an excuse to Helen and returned to his villa to sleep there quietly.

As he undressed he faced his problem. He could put it in two words—that Clark. He'd taken more than enough from Belami Clark and moreover he was still a menace. His arrogance and insults apart he knew far too much for peace of mind and he could if he wished to make trouble with policemen. Molina was determined he shouldn't. For Clark had been right, Molina was happy here. He meant to settle down in this villa and he didn't intend to do so alone. When Helen had finished her wretched mission . . .

That Clark again, there was no escaping him.

But there *was* a way and Molina had faced it. The problem was not what to do but how. How and of course the when and where. He had two servants who would kill if he told them, or, safer, he could still kill himself. He'd told Helen he could use a knife and using a knife on Clark would give pleasure. Alas that a knife also left a body and bodies, however carefully disposed of, had a disquieting habit of turning up later. He couldn't live in peace with Helen with a body in the garden or in the lake. So it would have to look like some casual mishap, he'd decided on that several days ago, and that was in one sense a plan of action. But it was the skeleton of a plan, not the flesh. . . . Take Clark out in a car and smash it up? But why should Clark agree to go with him, and where was any guarantee that he wouldn't kill himself as well? Or maim himself—he preferred the former. Or Clark was eating alone, he might have him poisoned. . . .

Out of some silly book. Forget it.

He took his problem to bed and he woke with the answer. He could kill Clark very simply indeed and no man could say that it wasn't misfortune. He could do it any day he chose at four o'clock in the afternoon.

It was just before dawn and still quite dark. Molina lit a cigarette since it wasn't worth while to sleep again. He lay quietly, thinking out the details.

Quite easy, very simple indeed. And he didn't need to hurry it. Even the most watertight plan could go wrong if you mistimed it rashly.

He had reached this conclusion when his bed shook perceptibly. Simultaneously the window rattled. He thought of an earthquake but turned that down. The Swiss would never permit an earthquake. No, it had been a muffled explosion and it seemed to have come from directly below him.

175

He took his knife from underneath his pillow and stole down the stairs on naked feet. The door of his study was open, faint light inside.

He was a smallish man and could move like a cat. He crept silently up to the door, watched as silently. There was the smell of some pungent chemical, no smoke. The door of his safe was standing open and Clark and the Dutchman were bending over it.

Molina was very sorely tempted. He was armed and possibly they were too but their hands were full and his own were free. Moreover their backs were turned. . . .

Three paces, a quick rush. They were dead. Once he'd been very fast with the knife.

He shook his head for it wasn't on. To begin with he'd just received enlightenment and it would be profane to fly in the face of it by acting on a sudden impulse. Profane and also most unwise, for there would still be two bodies and he'd have to account for them. In Switzerland a very rich man would get away with self defence, especially when the Swiss god of property was standing there outraged and insulted, but he couldn't prevent a police inquiry. Things would never be quite the same again.

Nevertheless he must change his programme. Evidently Clark needed money and Molina knew what his safe contained. Clark would be hoping for gold and Bearers, probably a large sum in cash, and Molina had plenty of those, all three of them. But he kept them at various banks, not at home. All the safe held was the housekeeping float, maybe a couple of hundred pounds, and some trinkets to sweeten female visitors. The trinkets would be hard to dispose of even if they had been of much value, and two hundred pounds

176

would go almost nowhere. If Clark was prepared to blow a safe his need must be both large and urgent.

Molina slipped away from the door: there was no point in risking their seeing him watching them. But away from it he went on thinking. So Clark needed money and needed it badly and there wasn't enough in the safe to serve him. What followed from that? It was very unpleasant. If Molina went back to bed they might follow him.

Extortion in most disagreeable forms, or maybe they'd do something wild like trying to kidnap Helen Monteath.

Helen—he must think of her too. He must get to her and do so at once. This wasn't running away, it was simply sensible. There was his man at her house but two would be better. Besides, he wasn't safe here himself. There was no point in facing pain unnecessarily.

He stole through the kitchen, still barefooted, and out across the yard to the garages. He took a car and drove away fast. There was a nip in the early morning air and Molina was still in his silk pyjamas, but as he drove to the chalet he sang gaily in Spanish. He had reason to be gay, he decided, for his problems had melted away like mist. Nominally he subscribed to the Faith, but he didn't believe that some saint or angel had sent him his recent revelation. It was deeper than that, much older and surer. And whatever it be it had done him proud, not only a solution of doubt but a friendly warning to change his timing. For he couldn't act at leisure now, coolly sitting back and choosing the moment. The pressure was on him. Very well, he would meet it.

This afternoon. This very day.

At the chalet the man he had posted challenged, but he let him pass when he saw who he was. Molina used his key and went upstairs. Helen was asleep in the bed and Molina crept in beside her quietly. She didn't wake and Molina was glad of it. He had work to do that afternoon and he needed to be at the top of his form.

13

Molina was eating breakfast with Helen in the alcove of the chalet's kitchen. He kept clothes there and was fully dressed in his normal manner of ease before elegance. Helen was fully dressed as well for she knew that below his air of casualness lay a streak of rather old-fashioned formality. A woman who ate in a dressing-gown would lose several points on his private scale. They were eating croissants and drinking good coffee which Helen had made in the well found kitchen. She looked around it, quiet and contented. The atmosphere was relaxed and domestic. They might have been a married couple, established some time but still pleased with the marriage. He made the early tea, she the breakfast. The window looked out on the charming small garden and the sun had begun to paint the flowers. Helen said happily: 'Will you be waterskiing?'

'Not till the afternoon as usual.'

'It's going to be a lovely day for it.'

'It needs to be a lovely day. Yesterday was a very bad one.'

He told her of Clark and the Dutchman robbing his safe. Helen Monteath at the end said uneasily: 'He must be desperate for money.'

'Yes. And I don't keep a lot in my safe. He found little.'

'Does that mean he could try again?'

'I'm afraid so.' He smiled at her with a hint of apology. 'That's why I'm here and I'll stay if you'll let me. He might try something *really* foolish.'

'Of course you can stay for as long as you like.'

'I hope it won't be all that long. I've a feeling the crisis is very near.' He held up his hand as she started to speak. 'No, don't tell me what I don't need to know. Your business and Charles Russell's isn't mine.'

'You've been more than helpful to both of us.'

'Good.'

He lit her cigarette, his own cigar, and they were smoking in understanding silence when the maid came in with a quick Swiss bustle.

'There's a man at the door and he says it's urgent.' She looked at Molina for he'd told her the drill. 'Your guard picked him up as he rang the bell but he gave me the signal he isn't armed.'

'Is he trying to sell us a vacuum cleaner?'

'No, I don't think so. He's not a salesman.'

'Did he give his name?'

'I can't pronounce it but he left a card.' The maid gave it to Helen Monteath politely. Helen read it and passed it across to Molina. He rose on a reflex but sat down again firmly. To the maid he said: 'Show him into the living-room.'

When the maid had gone Helen asked: 'Is that wise?'

Molina looked at the card reflectively. It was old and a little yellowed but clean. Belami Clark didn't often use visiting cards. 'There is every advantage. If he chooses to show his hand we should hear him.'

'We agreed he must be desperate.'

'Perfectly true. But he's also a very long way from stupid and any violence in this house would be silly.

Besides, if Miguel says he's unarmed he is.' He looked from the card to Helen Monteath, adding with a smile: 'Coming too?'

'Just try and stop me.'

'Nothing so foolish.'

In the living-room Belami Clark was standing. He was staring out of the window intently, his rigid back the clearest signal that he disapproved harshly of what he saw. The little garden showed care and money spent on it, and the room he had already inspected. He could see that it wasn't offensively grand, out of place in a modest summer chalet, but everything in it was good and expensive. It belonged to a world which Clark hated fiercely.

He turned as Molina and Helen came in. Molina said: 'Please sit down' and Clark did so. Molina's cigar was still alight; he found an ashtray and another for Helen but he did not suggest that Clark should smoke. He and Helen sat down on the sofa and waited.

'It is kind of you to receive me,' Clark said. He was trying for a tone of casualness but he only seemed tense and strained and desperate.

'I could think of a better adjective. Speak.'

'I imagine you've heard of your safe by now.'

'I didn't have to hear. I saw you.'

'You did? You were very quiet indeed.'

'I saw no point in risking a fracas. That safe held very little indeed.'

'As we found out.'

'So you've come here for more.'

He's deliberately making it easy, she thought. I wonder what game he's privately playing. I know that when he's pushed he's dangerous.

181

'Quite right,' Clark said.

'Two million pounds, for instance. You asked it before.'

'No, nothing as large as that today. I need five thousand pounds to see me over.'

'May I ask over what?'

'You may not.'

'As you will.' Molina considered. 'Not a vast sum,' he said at length.

'To you it's a fleabite.'

'Perhaps it is. But a flea with a poisoned tongue just the same. I can't say I greatly relish extortion.'

'You used the word first.'

'Of course I did. You would hardly come here and ask me for money unless you believed you had means to obtain it.'

Clark shrugged but began to disclose what these were. 'I told you before I had other resources, much more than just your couple of bodyguards. Now what could those do against well armed men?'

'Nothing,' Molina said; he was lying. His private but firm opinion was that they'd give anyone a fair run for his money. But this he did not say; he spread his hands. 'Nothing,' he repeated. 'Nothing.'

'That granted then you give me two choices.' Clark looked at Molina with open hatred. 'Are you good at pain?'

'I have suffered pain. I did not enjoy it.'

'You are thinking you might withstand real pain? I assure you you are mistaken. However . . . ' This time he looked at Helen Monteath. 'Of my two choices I prefer the lady.'

'Very unchivalrous.'

'Foolish comment. I am not, as you should know, a chivalrous man.'

'Paying blackmail is always stupid.'

'True. But the adage rests on a single assumption, that the alternative is to go to the police. And that, as we both know, you cannot do.' Behind the coolness was a compulsive urgency.

Molina seemed to be thinking it over; he asked at last mildly: 'Five thousand pounds?'

'In cash, of course.'

'In good Swiss francs?'

'In German marks. I need marks for my purpose.'

Molina's cigar had gone out and he threw it away. 'I will go to the bank this morning and get them.'

Helen started to speak but he silenced her instantly, turning back to Belami Clark almost pleasantly. 'Where would you like the money? And when?'

'At four o'clock this afternoon. You can bring it to the Aqua Club with you.'

'You're going there yourself?. Very well.'

There was a note in the voice which Clark missed fatally but Helen's sharper ear caught it clearly.

. . . Oh God, he's going to do something crazy.

Molina rose and Clark left them stiffly. When he had done so Helen said miserably. 'You know he's hooked you now for ever. He'll bleed you for the rest of your life.'

'What you say is very true—in most cases. In this one it's going to be rather different.'

'That's what they all hope.'

'I'm not hoping, I know.'

'Molina——' she began.

'May I use your telephone?'

He went to it and rang his villa, speaking to his distant cousin, the one he sometimes called his butler. He shared the watch on Helen's chalet with Miguel who was now on duty. That meant it was now the cousin's rest time, he'd need several hours' sleep and something to eat. Molina was a considerate master but this matter was of real importance. The cousin could manage a speedboat and Miguel couldn't.

So he gave his order clearly and crisply. The cousin was to go to the Aqua Club. At half-past three and that meant three-thirty. He was to take the speedboat and fuel her generously. Then he was to wait for Molina.

He put the receiver down and returned to Helen. She'd been thinking as he talked and asked him: 'I know you won't like it, but what about Russell?'

He shook his head at once. 'Not Russell. This is between myself and Clark, and in any case what could Russell do?'

She was distressingly conscious of being a woman. For all her meticulous training, her gun, she was a woman and Molina her man. Her breath was coming fast, her knees were jelly.

Molina was repeating sharply: 'Not Russell—I won't have him dragged into this. In fact I forbid you to tell him anything.'

'Very well,' she said weakly, 'but for God's sake take care.'

He took her hand and kissed it. 'The same with you. Because when I come back I'll·have something to ask of you.'

'Whatever you want.'

He was suddenly the old gay Molina.· 'It normally takes nine months, I believe.'

She was astonished but met his mood without showing it. 'Haven't you enough already?'

'Oh dozens and dozens—quite outrageous. But none I intend to give my name to.'

At three o'clock Helen broke her promise. She had eaten no lunch and was pushed to her limit, waiting in the sitting-room miserably for a call which she knew would never come. Molina wasn't the sort to change his mind.

And the room had suddenly got on her nerves. It didn't strike her as it had struck Belami Clark as a symbol of unmerited wealth, but the impeccable English county taste had begun to fray her temper cruelly, the chintz and the hunting prints, the bits of good china. It was almost clinical in its cool precision. It was better than Scots baronial where she'd spent unhappy and frustrated years, but when Molina came back she'd change it, she surely would.

When Molina came back. If Molina came back. Clark wasn't one to play foolish games with. And what was a promise when so much was at stake? She knew this was woman's thinking; she did not care.

She rose and rang the Bleiner, asked for Russell.

He'd been resting in a chair in pyjamas. 'You say he's going to his bank for the money? That doesn't sound like Molina.'

'It isn't.'

'And he's meeting Clark at four o'clock but he called up his man for half-past three?'

'At the Aqua Club. Both dates.'

'Then pick me up here at once. Immediate.'

'What do you plan to do?'

'I plan nothing. There isn't the time to interfere even

185

if we could read his mind.'

'Then what's the point of going?'

'As witnesses. Perhaps if something goes wrong we could somehow help. I can't promise more than that and I don't.'

'Shall I bring a gun?'

'Very well. If you must.' He said it a little wearily for he couldn't see any use for a gun. Whatever Molina was planning he'd carry out. A gun wouldn't stop him and surely not Helen's.

'I don't know how to thank you.'

'Don't.'

Russell rang off and dressed himself quickly. He recovered from any injury fast but he was wishing he were a decade younger.

The Colonel-General was briefing the man who would lead them, saying: 'You can see what's at stake.'

'Yes, Comrade General.'

'Stop calling me Comrade. It's as out of date as textbook Marxism.'

'Then, Yes sir.'

'That's better. So where had we got?'

'I was seeing what was at stake. But not clearly.'

'Damn it, man, it's as clear as sin.' Like Helen the General was near his limit but for reasons which were much less personal. For his earlier information was now confirmed. Troops *had* been moving, the excuse some exercise. That had been used before, had worn thin, but the General wasn't concerned with excuses; he was concerned with the movements and these couldn't be hidden. There was far too much flying the skies to allow it, too much tracking by highly developed devices. So the menace was now a double danger. He didn't underrate the Americans. Their allies wouldn't lift a finger, they'd go running like sheep making sheeplike noises, but the Americans might choose to preempt. He didn't put it past them. They had the means.

'I should have thought it was perfectly plain to a baby.' He knew he was being rude and regretted it but the strain had begun to increase with each hour. 'I've been given till Tuesday morning at latest to establish that what goes on at Neuwald is a single man's gigantic bluff. And it's clear that I can't do that and I never shall.' His voice changed suddenly: 'Did you fight in the war?'

'I was a child but I saw my parents die. Later the Germans took me to labour. There they starved me and hundreds of thousands of others.'

'Then if you thought they were making the Bomb?'

'I'd destroy them. There wouldn't be anything else to do.'

The Colonel-General nodded shortly. The answer had saved a political lecture. He must still recite the situation but could confine himself to events in Neuwald and to the outline of his plans to deal with them. It took him a full ten minutes to do so and at the end he said: 'Now questions, please.'

'I haven't any questions, sir.'

'You should have at least one so I'll answer it for you. This is very close timing indeed—most uncomfortable. The time I've been given expires on Tuesday so I've got to have your signal that morning. The ferry leaves the German side at round about midnight, perhaps a bit later. She'll be out in the middle at one or half past, which is half past four or five to us.

After that there'll be no drawing back.'

'It isn't exactly a question, sir, but if I signal these men are dead can you hold it? The soldiers, I mean. Another great war.'

'I wish I could guarantee that. I cannot. These things build up their own momentum and if somebody makes a slip there's a crash. But I'd hope for a very good chance, at least of time. I could, for a change, be clear and definite. I could say there was no *immediate* danger. Perhaps the heat would come off and perhaps it wouldn't.'

'Once I would have prayed.'

'I do still.'

The General relapsed into worried silence. He broke it to ask: 'You have this clear? You realize why we can't take the easy way? Clark's men are in that deserted house and it would be simple enough to kill them there. A quick in and out on sleeping men . . . . But Clark is still in Molina's villa with the Dutchman and they'll both be armed. A raid on an occupied villa, a shoot-up, would be something very different—too clumsy. Even the Swiss could hardly suppress it and the Swiss are very good at suppressing. So we'll have to wait till they're all together and we cannot be certain of that till Tuesday. Tuesday in the early morning. I don't like it, it cuts my own time to the bone, but I've considered it and I'll have to accept it. We must act when they're out on the water or never.'

'I don't like the sound of *their* plan. It's barbarous.'

The General said sharply: 'That's not for you. I'll run through the details—they're all that concern you. I've already chosen your team of four. All of them speak excellent German and all of them will have excellent passports. Three are also ex-Navy frogmen.'

'I understand that.'

'You will steal a boat?'

'If I couldn't steal a boat I shouldn't be here.'

'I stand reproved and accept it humbly. Here are your tickets.' He handed them over. 'It's an ordinary scheduled flight to Bonn, then on by another to Zurich airport. Hire a car normally, drive to Neuwald. The return date is of course left open, but if you run into trouble you make for Liechtenstein. You know where the safe house is. Lie up there.' The General rose. 'I wish you good luck.'

'May I wish you the same?'

'At this end? I may need it.'

When the leader had gone the General poured coffee. He was going to need the breaks, much luck, but at the worst he would be buying postponement. The machine was too big to stop dead in its tracks, but the barrels of guns cooled. So did men.

He finished his coffee and went to bed. It would keep him awake but he slept badly in any case. He lay and thought as Russell had, of the scene on the dark lake, its bleak horror. . . . Nothing to show it was other than accident. The sub-human snouts emerging obscenely, the murderous shower of grenades, the cries and the creeping remorseless flames.

The picture gave the General no pleasure. These men were his enemies, dangerous enemies, and as a soldier he had seen great slaughters. But he was also a fastidious killer. Melodramatic violence offended him.

On the telephone Molina had talked rapid idiomatic Spanish but Helen had picked up 'half-past three' and

189

she reached Russell at three-fifteen in a hurry. They drove to the Aqua Club totally silent, both busy with their different thoughts. Helen was scared for Molina's safety in some adventure he hadn't vouchsafed to explain, Russell apprehensive of trouble, the inevitable complications after any act by a man who'd been driven too far. As it sounded as if Molina had been. He had liked Molina, liked Helen more, and she'd dropped him a hint they had plans for the future. A pity if ill-considered action brought an outraged police on Molina's heels. He was a very rich man and this was Switzerland, but he couldn't use overt violence and walk away.

At the Aqua Club Helen ordered tea and they sat on the terrace outside to drink it. It was very nasty tea indeed and neither did more than sip it distastefully. Below them the lake was calm and placid, almost pretty for once in the afternoon sun, the colour of a bottle of Hock and with something of such a bottle's sheen. There was a single man beyond the basin, waterskiing with fair competence. Charles Russell had brought glasses and used them. He handed them to Helen.

'That's Clark.'

She used them in turn, then switched to the basin. 'I don't see any sign of Molina. He's usually so punctual and——'

There was a sudden stir in the basin below them. A man had started a speedboat's engine and another was climbing in with waterskis. He wore a wet suit and an air of purpose. Helen said: 'Molina'; was silent.

In the basin Molina's usual driver had been offended and had at first protested, but Molina had waved him brusquely aside. Normally polite to servants today he was thinking of only one thing. He stepped into the boat with his skis and the speedboat slipped out into open water.

'It's a beautiful day for it,' Helen said. She remembered she'd said the same thing at breakfast. 'But he can't be intending to pass money on waterskis.'

'His date with Clark was at four o'clock but he called up his man for half-past three. Does that convey anything?'

'Not very much. Except that he meant to waterski first.'

'And why should he do that?'

'He loves it.'

They took it in turns to use Russell's glasses. Molina had slipped over the side and his cousin was leaning over it, listening. They couldn't hear what Molina said but in fact he was rehearsing his driver.

'You understood what I told you?'

The cousin nodded.

'Kindly repeat it.'

'*Si, señor*. When you hold up your right arm I steer to the right. Similarly with your left—to the left. If you touch your head I slow a little but if you strike your breast I go full out.' He passed out the rope but Molina declined it.

'The wire today,' he said, 'it's stronger.'

He was up on his skis at once but cruising, running parallel to Belami Clark. They turned at the end of the authorized run, then both started the return, still parallel. The distance between them was fifteen yards.

'Aren't they a little close?' Russell asked.

'Molina is very careful indeed.'

It suddenly hit him: Russell rose but sat down again.

Belami Clark was going to die.

The pace had become a little faster and Molina suddenly held his right arm up. His driver went right and Molina followed, outside the boat's wake in a flowing arc. He missed Belami Clark by perhaps two feet.

Helen Monteath said: 'Oh God.' Russell nothing.

Clark had teetered but somehow stayed upright, still skiing. Molina had moved away a little and for a hundred yards they were once more parallel. Parallel but now very much closer. Molina raised his right arm again and as he lowered it he struck his chest. He crouched and his driver opened the throttle.

Molina swung at Clark again but this time his arc took him slightly outside him. He was moving up on Clark's right, flat out. For a second Clark could see his face. If he'd lived he would have remembered it always.

But he didn't live. He fell off instead. Molina felt the searing wrench, then the wire went limp as he let it go.

He sank into the water expertly, releasing his skis and swimming strongly. He swam to what was left of Clark. The body was floating, the head had sunk.

It was odd, Molina thought—very odd. The body was floating in almost clear water. So the books which he'd always mistrusted were right. Once the heart stopped beating there wasn't much blood.

He signalled to his speedboat and climbed in.

14

Helen was lunching with Russell gaily. The Bleiner hadn't improved its food but they'd had several drinks before to wash it down. Over the third of them Helen said: 'The police have called on Molina. You can guess.'

'I think I can guess their line but you tell me.'

'You said something about your being a witness but I hardly think that's going to be necessary. They talked about the equivalent of driving on the road very dangerously. They were severe all right but never menacing.'

'For how could they prove that it wasn't an accident?'

'That's exactly the impression they gave—some suspicion but no intention of action. But they made all the points at tedious length. Why had Molina taken his servant instead of the boatman he usually uses? In fact he'd taken him for his inexperience, because he couldn't have realized what Molina was up to till it was too late to change and then he wouldn't have. He's Molina's cousin, intensely loyal. So Molina just said that he wanted to train him; he even talked about saving money. He can be very cool indeed, as you know.'

'Had they spoken to this cousin first?'

'Of course. But Molina had told him nothing whatever so he hadn't a thing to tell the police, except he'd been given a code of signals. That's perfectly normal with new drivers of speedboats. They have to know what their tow expects of them and there's too much noise on the water to shout.'

'Very neat,' Charles Russell said. 'Well thought out. And did they ask about Belami Clark himself?'

'Certainly, and Molina told them. He'd been Adviser when Molina was President, he'd saved his life in the revolution, and now he was his guest in Neuwald. The police can check all that and it's perfectly true.' She laughed happily. 'As far as it goes and that isn't far. Anything else is between ourselves.'

'What then?' Russell asked.

'Then they turned on the heavy stuff. Molina, by all accounts, was accomplished and he was normally exemplarily careful, but yesterday he'd been skiing dangerously. To whip a man's head off like that—disgraceful. They were funny about that—very Swiss. At one moment they were pretty tough. It appears you don't need a licence to waterski but they said that if you did they'd cancel it. At the next they were all over him, talking about his special status, his position as an honoured guest. It was clear that they knew he was very rich.'

'How did it end?'

'Not too well for Molina. They asked him to promise not to ski again, at any rate for several months till the affair had had some time to blow over. After that they might perhaps reconsider, but they'd have to put the decision much higher.'

'He accepted that?'

'Of course he did. He isn't a man to push his luck. He knew they couldn't prove a thing and financially it wouldn't pay them to try, but they could still make his life extremely uncomfortable if he set them against him by giving wrong answers. So he agreed though I could see he hated it. Waterskiing is half his life.'

'And the other half?'

'An indiscreet question.'

'I beg your pardon.' Charles Russell thought. 'Another little drink?'

'I think I will.'

When it came he asked: 'And the other matter?'

'What other matter?'

'You're not as naive as that.'

'But I am.' She said it with evident satisfaction. 'I'm naive as the girl of sixteen I feel. My head's in a whirl——'

'Better brake it down.'

'So Molina and I have been out to that house.'

'Utter and incredible folly.'

'I'm sorry, I'm getting the sequence wrong. We knew it was empty. It was perfectly safe.'

'For heaven's sake tell the story straight.'

'All right, I'll try, though I think I'm high. Less with drink, I think, than——'

'For God's sake go on.'

'So last night I went back to Molina's villa since there wasn't any danger from Clark. The Dutchman had heard the news, I suppose, for there wasn't a trace of him high or low. We went to Clark's room and searched it. In a cupboard was a short-wave radio.'

'The pair to the other one up at the house?'

'I supposed so when we found it and I was right.' She added in almost her normal manner: 'I don't think Clark used it very much—the police might pick it up or some ham. So we took the thing to our sinful bed and at two in the morning it woke us up.'

'A timed call?'

'I think so. Somebody was talking Spanish and I left it to Molina to answer. But I can understand the odd word of Spanish.'

'What did they say?'

'They asked for Clark. Molina said he was dead. There was panic.'

'Understandably. And so?'

'More panic—they'd left the channel open. The Dutchman was there, I could hear him shouting. He was bawling in Dutch which I don't understand but he was also shouting in German which I do. Finally he got his way. He has a very loud voice and he's very Dutch. You know what a shouting Dutchman is like.'

'I admire the Dutch,' Russell said, 'but I follow you.'

'His way was almost English—a compromise. He'd heard something on the public radio about an accident to Clark on the lake and that is why he'd gone off to the others. But the authorities were still being cagey and the radio didn't confirm actual death. So the Dutchman would wait till six o'clock and if Clark didn't call by then they'd be off. Molina and I knew he couldn't call so at seven we went off to the house. I remember it was a beautiful morning.'

'Damn the weather, woman. What did you find?'

'We found, as you would expect, just nothing.'

'The armoury had gone too?'

'It had. Presumably it's out in the lake. Arms are difficult things to bring across frontiers.'

'Somebody, sooner or later, is going to find traces.'

'That the house has been inhabited—yes. So they'll tell the police who will say it was squatters.'

196

'No actual identification?'

'None. And I assure you that we looked pretty carefully.'

Russell fell into silence, a little doubtful. Not at what Helen had told him: that was clear. He was doubtful of his own emotions. . . . So those clowns had got away. Convenient. If they'd been taken they could have talked disastrously, and their talking would have blown wide open what Russell and his friend the General had always had the best motives to hide. Clark had been the head and fount and Clark had obliged Molina to kill him. Let the small fry go, they could still cause much mischief, but who in this brash and beastly world had a watertight right to condemn them utterly?

Charles Russell frowned for this wouldn't do. There was only one word for that: it was casuistry.

This decided he returned to Helen. 'You've reported to the General, of course?'

'Who sent me a rather curious answer. He thanked me for the hand I'd dealt him. He said that it wasn't a lay-down slam but it would certainly keep the game open a while.'

'He'll probably send you a medal.'

'No. For I've also given in my notice. Just like a char.' She almost giggled.

'Will he accept it?'

'I think he'll have to. I know too much if the man turned nasty but hardly enough to be worth a killing.'

'I don't think he's the nasty kind.'

'I'm very glad you think so too.'

'You've worked it all out.'

'I mean to stay here.'

'Yes,' Russell said, 'yes, I rather thought so.' He

looked at her empty plate with approval. She had eaten like a horse in a famine. 'Will you take a glass of brandy now?'

'I'm a little drunk already, you know.'

'That I can see but I'll drive you home.'

'Home is Molina's villa. Consider that. . . . Charles Russell arrives with Molina's woman and the woman is something more than tiddly——'

'Molina is a sensible man. Sober I find you extremely attractive, a little tiddly you would restore my youth.'

'You're very gallant.'

'I'm also practical.'

He signalled to the winewaiter firmly.

In the oval room they were talking again but this time the second man was in uniform. He wore rather more medals and decorations than an Englishman would have considered seemly except on the most formal occasion but he knew his business and he spoke with authority.

'For the moment we think any danger is off.'

'Why? Have they moved the troops back?'

'Not yet. But they've moved back their petrol and in some ways that's better.'

'I'm not sure I get it.'

The soldier explained. 'Petrol in tankers is dangerously vulnerable but an armoured attack can't get far without it. They'd rely on transporters as far as they dared, then the tanks would be on their own with what they held.' He looked at a paper. 'Say two hundred miles, give a little each way. And two hundred miles is not enough.'

'Where's the fuel gone?'

'Back to hardened storage.'

'You're sure of that?'

'As sure as we can be. Nothing is ever certain in war.'

'War,' the man behind the desk repeated. 'The last of the wars.' He was thinking that he wouldn't be tested though he knew what he would have done if he'd had to. 'And the troops?' he asked. 'The concentrations of infantry?'

'They won't be withdrawn in a day or even a month. That's a matter of face and accordingly sensitive. There'll be some sort of major exercise, which is what they always said they intended, then they'll quietly go back to their normal bases.'

'Your professional opinion?'

'Yes sir.'

The man behind the desk stood up; he shook hands with the man in uniform pleasantly. 'Till the next time,' he said.

'Till the next time, God help us.'

And far to the east in a different country the Colonel-General was sitting alone. He was extremely grateful to Helen Monteath and had no intention of making difficulties. Women agents could seldom be useful for long and she had more than earned a pleasant retirement. The last news she had sent him had loosened his hook—not removed it completely, he knew that well—but it had brought him what he most needed. Time. And he knew how to use that time and where. He'd told Russell that there were hawks and doves, and now with any luck the doves might win. He couldn't give reassurances but now perhaps he needn't do so. Belami Clark was dead, the small fry gone. He needn't think of frogmen and pools of flame.

But he must send a final signal to Russell. Partly to thank him, he'd more than earned that, but there was also a single loose end to tidy. Russell would have noticed it too and Russell would take steps to knit it, but there was no harm in letting a friend know discreetly that an old enemy still knew his trade.

Molina had called on his doctor again. He was dressed with an unusual formality for he had a formal appointment later that morning. It was one at the town hall and important. 'I want another shot,' he said.

'That stuff can kill you.'

'You mean it's a poison?'

'Of course it isn't a poison. Rubbish. I mean the law of lesser returns, my friend. If I go on pumping it into you there'll come a time when it won't be of very much use. And then where will the busy bee go for honey?'

'But I intend to get married.'

'Congratulations.' The doctor reflected. 'Ever married before?'

Molina shook his head with decision.

'I rather thought not. Then a word of advice. Marriage is a little different from keeping an oriental harem.'

'How did you know about that?'

'I hear things.'

'Then how is marriage different?'

The doctor, who was married, sighed. 'You want it to last?'

'Of course I do.'

'You intend to raise a family?'

'Certainly.'

'As you stand you can do that with something to

spare. Come back in nine months if you feel a bit jaded.'

'Is that a deal?'

'It's a deal.'

'Very well.'

Molina drove back to the villa briskly. He had given Helen a room of her own and she was furnishing it to suit herself. Not the austerities of a broken-down castle nor the faintly fussy good taste of the chalet she'd left. She was going to be here some time. . . . How long? Well, Molina had done more than hint but he hadn't yet come out in the open.

He came in and gave her a diamond ring. It was enormous and had cost much money, and there were tastes which would have considered it vulgar. Molina knew this but he didn't consider it. When he did a thing he did it properly. As he put it on her hand he asked: 'Are you a Roman Catholic?'

'No.'

'I still am, I suppose, but not a good one. I haven't been near a priest for years and I threw out the Jesuits neck and crop.'

She had a dozen questions to ask but knew better. In his present mood they would only annoy him. But one was still fair and she put it pleasantly: 'Why do you ask?'

'For the obvious reason. You might have wanted a marriage in church.'

'All in white?'

He grinned. 'I think we can manage without the white. In any case there isn't time. Our appointment is at twelve o'clock.'

She said what any woman would have. 'But I haven't any clothes——'

Molina sat down on the sofa and laughed at her. 'Women,' he said, 'I'm delighted they're different.'

'But you've put a suit on yourself.'

'I know. What do you want, a morning coat? Or full evening dress with the orders I gave myself?'

'I only want to do you justice.'

'Fiddle. But I love you dearly.' It was the first time he'd ever said it in words. He looked at his watch. 'But I'll tell you what. There's two hours before noon for a little brisk shopping. You can change at the Bleiner. I'll fix a room.'

'You mean it?'

'I mean what I say though I'm slow at saying it. Including,' he added softly, 'nine months.'

'I heard you the first time but make it ten. Give me a little margin.'

'Done. Then nine and a half at the most. No fooling.'

The General had been right as usual: there was still a loose end and Charles Russell had noticed it. It was a man called James Campbell with a curious story, one which could cause rather more than embarrassment. Charles Russell had considered this carefully. James Campbell wasn't a talkative man but he'd suffered what was undoubtedly outrage and it would be natural if he sought a remedy. So Russell had been phoning discreetly. He was retired but he still had powerful connections and he'd found what he wished to know quite easily. James Campbell was coming up for his Knighthood and Campbell would almost certainly know of it.

Charles Russell nodded, entirely satisfied. James Campbell could start a resounding scandal, cause much trouble to men who had plenty already, men who would resent it bitterly. But the New Year's Honours were five months distant, and men who had hopes of seeing their names there would do nothing to put those hopes at risk. Certainly not start an uproar. That was the way this strange world worked.

Russell saw Campbell off at the airport. He was travelling with Molina's cousin though he'd insisted he didn't need an attendant. But Molina had been adamant. It was in Molina's house that Campbell had suffered and from that house he must leave in proper style. If he wouldn't accept the cousin as company Molina would have to go himself and at this moment that would be most inconvenient.

Campbell had given way at last and Charles Russell saw him onto the aircraft.

'A distressing little adventure,' he said.

'You're extremely good at understatement.'

'One better forgotten.'

'I shall never forget it.' He gave Russell his dour but pleasant smile. 'I shall never forget it and nobody else will. They won't have the chance to forget. They won't hear.'

'I know people who'll be very grateful. I would guess that they'd show their gratitude handsomely.'

James Campbell said: 'The old Adam still——'

'Not at all—I'm retired. But I still have friends.'

'So I'm entitled to gather. Goodbye.'

Russell went back to the Bleiner and packed. He was catching an evening flight to Vienna. It doubled the distance back to England but there was good motive behind the apparent folly. Though he flattered himself he didn't show it the last few days had been days of strain, to say nothing of that damned Japanese, and there was nothing like one of the world's great trains to relax a man to his normal urbanity. The well trained service, the respectable food—after the Bleiner's much more than respectable—the sense of majestically sweeping the night aside as you lay in your *wagon lit* and drowsed. Such a train was Russell's proven restorative.

Nor did it let him down when he caught it. The food was what he'd expected, edible, and the wine, though not up to the General's standards, was better than in most English restaurants.

He went back to his berth and put on pyjamas. The blue nightlight glowed with a quiet reassurance.

. . . I have only to press that bell and a servant . . . God damn it, I'm in the womb again, any need I can think of met without question.

Not quite, he decided regretfully. No. One thorn remained to pester insistently and there was nothing he could do to ease it. Across the western world the piles burned fiercely. Uranium into plutonium, back again. Perhaps he hadn't got that quite right, he was ignorant. That wasn't a matter of great importance since even Clark hadn't dared to steal directly. Clark had been an aberration but Germany was awash with plutonium, the future Sir James had said so in terms. So probably were other states, but they were states with a long tradition behind them—civilized, for the little that meant. But what happened when some ape in Africa . . .

Russell seldom talked to himself but now he did. Unknowingly he repeated the soldier, the smooth adviser in the oval room. He said as he fell asleep: 'Till the next time.'